A moment later the front ⬤
Mrs. Benson. Alice, who had gone into her office,
popped back out t

"Hello and w
shake her hand.
usual ponytail an
prints across it, was great at putting both people and
dogs at ease. Which was good, because I realized that
tough-as-nails Mrs. Benson actually looked nervous.
And then I saw why. The little dog she was carrying
was stiff as a board in her arms.

Roxbury Park • D🐶g Club

Roxbury Dog Club

ALL PAWS ON DECK

DAPHNE MAPLE

HARPER

An Imprint of HarperCollinsPublishers

Roxbury Park Dog Club #4: All Paws on Deck

Text by Daphne Maple, copyright © 2016 by HarperCollins Publishers

Illustrations by Annabelle Metayer, copyright © 2016
by HarperCollins Publishers

www.harpercollinschildrens.com

ISBN 978-0-06-232773-4 (pbk.)

Typography by Jenna Stempel

16 17 18 19 20   OPM   10 9 8 7 6 5 4 3 2 1

First Edition

For Julia

1

"I've graded your tests," my English teacher, Mrs. Benson, said crisply. The bell for first period had barely finished ringing but she was already starting class and everyone, even Dennis Cartwright, class trouble-maker, was sitting down quietly. Mrs. Benson had that effect on people. It wasn't like she yelled or made scary threats. She just had this look that made you want to do your very best for her.

Which was why I was biting my lip as she began

passing back our papers. I really *had* done the best I could. But we'd just finished a biography of Marie Curie and even though it was pretty interesting, I'd gotten a little confused during Mrs. Benson's lectures about it. I'd try to take notes but she talked so fast that I'd still be writing down the first thing she said while she was already onto a whole other subject. And then I'd be so lost I wouldn't know what to write. My notebook was a mess of scribbles that didn't even make sense. Plus sometimes the book got a little confusing. Which was why I'd probably done pretty badly on this test. And that was not going to make my parents happy at all.

Mrs. Benson set a paper in front of my best friend Sasha, who looked at it and grinned. It wasn't so long ago that Sasha was the one having trouble with her homework, but not because she didn't understand it. She'd just gotten so busy with the Dog Club we'd started, and the dance classes she took after school—plus the new dog she'd adopted from the shelter where we had the club. But Taylor, our other best friend, and I had helped

Sasha figure out how to manage her time a little better and judging from the expression on Sasha's face, it was definitely working.

I saw Taylor give Sasha a small thumbs-up, so she must have noticed too. Then both of them looked at me just as Mrs. Benson put my paper on my desk. She'd set it facedown and just seeing that made my stomach twist. Good grades came face up. I took a breath and turned the paper over slowly. A bright red 68 was scrawled at the top.

My face felt hot and my eyes prickled. My parents had told me how important that test was and I'd promised them I'd study every night. And I had. But I'd still done terribly.

"It's okay, Kim," Sasha whispered sympathetically. Only the best of friends would risk a Mrs. Benson look by talking in class.

I tried to smile at Sasha but the corners of my mouth wouldn't cooperate. The red 68 made smiling impossible.

"So that concludes our unit on biographies," Mrs. Benson said. She was back at the front of the room, her hand resting on the pile of books on her desk. "And now we move on to one of my very favorite books, *The Adventures of Tom Sawyer.* Kwan, Danny, and Taylor, would you please help me pass these out?"

When Taylor set the book on my desk she reached over and squeezed my arm. The beads at the ends of her braids clinked gently as she moved down the aisle, and my skin still felt warm where she'd touched me. The 68 still ate at me but it helped to have Taylor and Sasha.

So I did the only thing I could. I opened my notebook and got ready to write down everything Mrs. Benson had to say about *Tom Sawyer.*

As soon as the bell rang Taylor and Sasha came over to me.

"Don't worry, you'll do better on the next one," Sasha said, pushing a dark brown curl out of her face. Sasha usually wore her hair back in a ballet bun or braid, but curls were always springing free as if they had a life of their own.

"Yeah, it's just one test," Taylor added. She was wearing a bright pink T-shirt that made her dark brown skin glow.

"I wish my parents thought that," I said as we headed into the crowded hallway. It was our first year at Roxbury Park Middle School and so far it had been going well, at least the part that didn't involve English. Or math, another subject where I was barely keeping up. But at least we had our community service project. At the beginning of seventh grade, we all had to sign up for an after-school volunteer job, and the three of us worked at the Roxbury Park Dog Shelter. That was how we'd come up with the idea for our Dog Club. It was also where Taylor and I had become friends. When she first moved to town at the start of the year, after her family spent a month of vacation with Sasha and her mom, I wasn't exactly happy to see her. Not that she wasn't nice, but she and Sasha had all these inside jokes and I felt like a third wheel. Sasha did everything she could to bring us together, but in the end it was a big dog named Boxer who made me see what Sasha had always known: Taylor was awesome. It had been the three of us ever since.

Taylor put her arm around me. "We'll help you study for the next one," she said.

"Oh, that's okay," I said automatically. I knew they wanted to help but they were both super busy, plus this was something I needed to figure out on my own. If everyone else in my class could do well on these tests, I could too. I just needed to try harder. "But thanks."

"We're here if you need us," Sasha said, patting my shoulder. "Oh, and I got an email this morning from another family interested in the Dog Club."

That was good news. Not so long ago we'd been struggling to find enough clients to make money to help the shelter—and that was the whole reason we'd started the club in the first place. When we'd first begun volunteering there, we'd quickly realized that the shelter had real financial problems. In fact, Alice, who ran it, had been forced to consider closing down. At the same time my neighbors, the Cronins, had been asking me about walking their dog, a sweet basset hound named Humphrey, after school. I couldn't help them because of my work at the shelter on top of my homework, but then I came up with a solution to both problems: the Roxbury Park Dog Club. It was simple, really. Dogs whose owners were busy at work could come to the shelter in the afternoon to play with the dogs there, and of course with us and the other shelter volunteers. The Cronins were our first clients but others soon followed and the club took off. There had been a few bumps along the way, like Clarabelle, the poodle who got muddy in the shelter yard right after an expensive grooming. And Sierra, a dog too wild for us to control. But we'd handled those problems and we, or to be more exact, Taylor, had found a way to fix things when we didn't have enough clients.

"Mrs. Halifax said she and her husband saw your

pictures in the paper," Sasha said, grinning at Taylor. "As soon they saw them they wanted to sign their dog up for the club." Two weeks ago there had been a photo spread of our Dog Club in the Sunday magazine, with some of the gorgeous shots Taylor had taken for our club blog. Our phone hadn't stopped ringing since! Well, Sasha's phone really. She was the one who handled new clients so Alice sent all messages straight to her. My job was to write the blog and Taylor made it beautiful with her doggy pictures. Together we really were an unbeatable team.

"Did you make an appointment for them to bring their dog by?" Taylor asked.

"They said they'd call back to schedule a time," Sasha said. "Which is good because we're pretty booked up." Before we accepted any new dogs into the club, we made an appointment for them to come in, along with their owners, to get a sense of what we did. That way we could make sure the dog and Dog Club were a good fit.

"What kind of dog do they have?" Taylor asked.

Sasha grinned. "A Saint Bernard," she said. "And apparently she's still a puppy."

"Whoa," Taylor said. "That's a big puppy."

"I know," Sasha agreed. "But we have our secret weapon if she gets wild."

They both looked at me and I felt my cheeks get warm, this time in a good way. My friends and family called me a dog whisperer. I wasn't sure if I really was, but I did understand dogs in a way that I couldn't fully explain. I knew what they wanted or needed just by looking at them and listening to the sounds they made. It was like I spoke their doggy language. Maybe it was just because they could tell I loved them so much, but whatever it was, it made me happy to be able to help dogs when they needed it. And puppies, especially the big ones, usually needed a little assistance staying calm.

The warning bell rang.

"See you guys later," Taylor said, giving me one last squeeze before heading off down the hall.

9

I waved to her and Sasha, then headed to my second-period class. The 68 still had my stomach in knots but my friends helped a lot and so did thinking about Dog Club. Because at least *that* was something I was good at.

2

The next day when the final bell rang I headed to my locker and began stuffing books into my back-pack. Sasha came over just as I was zipping it up. She'd had a dentist appointment this morning and missed lunch, so this was the first time I'd seen her all day.

"Ready for Dog Club?" I asked. My locker was between hers and Taylor's, so we always met up here and then headed out together.

"Yes, and I have some interesting news about our new client, the one who signed up last week," Sasha said, her cheeks pink. Sasha had pale skin, so whenever she was excited her cheeks got all rosy. "I'll tell you as soon as Taylor gets here."

"Sounds good," I said, heaving my bag onto my shoulders. After the test yesterday I was being extra careful in all my classes, so I was bringing most of my books home. It was a heavy load, but with an afternoon of doggy love to look forward to, I barely felt it.

"I wonder what's keeping Taylor," Sasha said, glancing at her phone to check the time. Now that school was over we could have cell phones out.

"It's not like her to be late," I said. "Should we text her?"

Just then Taylor rounded the corner and when I saw who had kept her, I felt a prickle of anxiety. Taylor was walking with Brianna Chen. Not so long ago Brianna had been mean to Taylor, mocking her clothes and making snide remarks about Taylor being the new girl.

To make matters worse, Brianna's mom's dog grooming salon, the Pampered Puppy, opened a new doggy day care and tried to put our Dog Club out of business. At least that was how it felt when they started posting negative ads about our club and we began losing clients to them. But Taylor's older sister Anna helped Taylor realize that Brianna was bothering Taylor because she was jealous of her. Brianna had been the new girl the year before and she had not had an easy time settling in. So Taylor, who is kind and generous, reached out to Brianna, telling her that she understood how hard things were for her. Brianna apologized for the mean things she had done and even got her mom to back off her ad campaign. Taylor had forgiven her but I wasn't so sure we could trust her. And by the way Sasha stiffened up next to me, I could tell she felt the same way.

"Hey," Taylor said, smiling happily when she saw us. She looked relaxed and cheerful.

Brianna smiled at us shyly. "Hi," she said, brushing back a lock of long black hair. Brianna was Asian, with tanned skin and thick black hair that fell nearly to her waist. Today she had it held back with a braided purple headband that went perfectly with her turquoise sweater and black leggings. "Are you guys going to the shelter?"

"Yeah," Sasha said, twisting a curl around her finger.

"It sounds really great there," Brianna said a little wistfully. "Taylor was telling me you guys play dog basketball. I have no idea what that is but it sounds fun."

That made me laugh. "Yeah, Tim, one of the high school volunteers, invented it," I said.

"It's very high tech," Taylor joked. "We have a laundry basket for the hoop."

"My mom would never do something like that at the Pampered Puppy," Brianna said.

I tensed up, not liking the way it sounded like she thought the game wasn't good enough for her mom's doggy day care.

But Taylor just laughed. "That's why it's so great our town has two doggy day cares," she said. "That way owners can get exactly what they want."

Brianna was nodding and I realized she hadn't been putting down our club at all. "Totally," she said.

"You'll have to come by and see it sometime," Taylor said.

"That would be really cool," Brianna said. "Now I should get to the library, not that anyone will notice if I'm late."

She must have been doing her volunteer work there, like a lot of other kids I knew.

"See you tomorrow," Taylor called as Brianna headed down the hall and the rest of us walked toward the big front doors of the school.

"Bri is going to sit with us at lunch tomorrow," Taylor announced cheerfully.

Sasha glanced at me, one brow raised, and I raised mine right back.

"Are you sure that's such a great idea?" Sasha asked as we walked down the steps. The sun was bright and a brisk wind perfumed with the smell of fall leaves was blowing.

"Of course," Taylor said, like it was no big deal.

"She seems nice and everything," I said. "But it wasn't so long ago that she was being pretty mean to you."

Taylor linked arms with both of us. "I know you guys are just looking out for me, but honestly, Bri is great. She's sorry for how she acted before and that's not who she is, not really."

It was true that Brianna had been nothing but sweet since she and Taylor made up, but that didn't mean I forgave her, not completely. And I could tell by the way Sasha was frowning that she felt the same way.

"You'll see," Taylor said, squeezing our arms. "She'll sit with us at lunch and I know you guys will learn to like her as much as I do."

"Okay," I agreed. I wasn't sure I trusted Brianna but I did trust Taylor. Plus I'd rather have Brianna around all of us together, so that Sasha and I could make sure she really was treating our friend right.

"So what did you have to tell us?" I asked Sasha, remembering that she said there was news about the client coming in this afternoon.

"Well, Alice told me about this client a few days ago—she asked to speak with Alice first because her dog has special circumstances," Sasha said. We stopped and waited as a truck went by before crossing Elm Street and heading toward town. "She just adopted a dog who was rescued from a puppy mill."

Those two words made my stomach drop. Animals at puppy mills were treated as breeding machines and newborn dogs were trapped in small wire cages with no human contact. It was cruel and I hated even thinking about it. "It's great this new client is giving one of those puppies a home," I said. That was the good part of the story.

"Yeah, and I know Alice told her about you and how you'd be able to help this puppy adapt," Sasha said, smiling at me.

I felt a warm glow at her words.

"But here's the surprise," Sasha went on. "The new client is Mrs. Benson!"

For a second I wasn't sure who she meant but then I gasped. "Wait, our English teacher?" I asked.

"Yeah," Sasha said. "Pretty wild, right?"

"Yeah," I agreed, my mind racing.

"Two worlds collide when shelter life meets school life," Taylor said in a television-announcer voice that usually made me laugh. But now I was just trying to wrap my mind around what it would be like to have crisp, intimidating Mrs. Benson at the shelter.

"It's pretty cool she rescued a puppy in need," Taylor said in her regular voice.

It definitely was. But what would it be like to work with Mrs. Benson outside of the classroom? I wasn't sure I wanted to find out.

"Hey, and that reminds me, Kim," Sasha said. "What did your parents say about the English test last night?"

"It was weird," I said, scuffling my feet through a small pile of leaves on the sidewalk. "They barely said anything. No pep talks or study hints or anything."

"That's good, right?" Taylor said.

18

"I guess," I said. "I mean, I'm glad they didn't say I might have to cut down on my hours at the shelter." They had said that after my last math test. "And I did promise that I'd do better next time."

"It sounds like they have faith that you will," Sasha said. We were approaching the intersection of Market and Grove, where we'd separate to get the club dogs. For a small fee we'd go pick up club dogs at their homes and walk them to the shelter for the afternoon. It was convenient for busy owners and helped us earn a little extra for the shelter.

"Yeah, now I just have to make sure that I study hard," I said. My stomach twisted at the thought. I'd studied hard for the last test and it hadn't gotten me very far.

"You'll do great," Sasha said encouragingly.

"And you can always ask Mrs. Benson for tips when she comes to the shelter," Taylor joked.

"That is going to be really weird," Sasha said as we reached the corner.

I totally agreed.

"See you in a few minutes," I said, heading off to pick up Humphrey and Popsicle, who happened to live right next door to me.

Popsicle, a fast-growing black and white puppy, bounced around joyfully when I let myself into their house. Humphrey waddled over to me, then threw himself down at my feet with a sigh, as though the walk from the living room to the front hall had exhausted him. Typical basset behavior that always made me smile.

"Hey, guys," I said, snuggling both of them before leashing them up and heading back into the sunny afternoon. "Now we're going to go get Mr. S." My older brother, Matt, sometimes made fun of the way I talked to dogs but I knew they understood me. Maybe not the exact words, but dogs were smart and very sensitive to tone of voice. And both Humphrey and Popsicle knew who Mr. S was.

Mr. S was Sasha's dog, recently adopted from the shelter. Since Sasha lived two houses down from the Cronins, whoever picked up Humphrey and Popsicle usually also got Mr. S. We liked to mix up who got which dogs so that we could all spend a little walking time with each of our clients.

Mr. S was a Cavachon who was nearly blind, not that you'd know it when he raced right over to us and began running in circles around Popsicle, creating a knot of leashes. "Hey, sweet boy," I said as I untangled everyone.

I snapped Mr. S's leash to his collar and we were on our way. A few minutes later we were walking into the shelter.

"Hey, Kim," Caley called out. She was one of the high school volunteers and she was playing fetch with Boxer, who was of course a boxer, and Lily, a shaggy tan mix. Following close behind on short little legs was Daisy, a brown dachshund whose owner dropped her off for club time each week. As soon as I unleashed Popsicle she ran to join the fun while Humphrey headed over to sniff a squeaky toy in the shape of a bone that was one of his favorites.

"Hi, Tim," I said to the other high school volunteer, who was on the floor playing tug-of-war with Waffles, the newest resident of the shelter. After our beloved Hattie, a shy sheepdog puppy, had been adopted a few weeks ago, Waffles had come in to take her place. Hattie was now a club dog, so we still got to see her, and Waffles, a cocker spaniel mix, had settled happily into life at the shelter.

"Hey, Kim," Tim said, brushing his black hair out of his eyes with his free hand. "What's new?"

For a moment I thought of my terrible English test, but that was the last thing I wanted to talk about here. "Not much," I said.

The door flew open and Sasha, her cheeks pink, came in with Hattie and Gus, a sweet chocolate brown Lab. Both bounded over to play as soon as their leashes were unhooked.

A moment later Taylor appeared with Coco, a big brown and black dog and the final club member— at least until Mrs. Benson arrived with her dog, a thought that made my chest tighten.

"Hi, everybody," Alice said coming out of her office, a little room at the front of the shelter. She was with Gracie, another shelter dog. "This girl now has nicely trimmed nails," she announced as Gracie ran up to me to say hello.

I gave her a big hug and she wriggled happily in my arms. "Want to play?" I asked her after a moment.

Gracie barked in response. I went over to the bins of toys that were stored on the shelves along one wall of the shelter. The other wall was lined with cages that each had a soft doggy bed and blanket. That was where the dogs slept but they were always open during the day in case a dog wanted to take a nap or spend a little quiet time alone. The main room of the shelter was big and open, with a new linoleum floor. There was a small bathroom off to one side, as well as the room where the dog food was stored, though the dogs were usually fed after we left.

"Want your green ball?" I asked Gracie. She pranced

at my feet until I tossed it across the room. Then she raced after it, Mr. S and Hattie right behind her.

"I think I'll take some of these rascals outside," Tim said, standing up and brushing off his shirt, which was now dotted with dog fur. "You guys want to join me?"

"We have a new client coming, so we should probably wait for her," Sasha said. Sasha, Taylor, and I tended to stick together at the shelter. And everywhere else too.

"Sounds good," Tim said. "It'll be better for the new dog if it's a little less hectic in here."

"Good point," I said. Of course the new dog would have to adjust eventually, but it would be nice if she wasn't overwhelmed the first moment she came through the door.

Tim and Caley headed outside with Boxer, Coco, Lily, and Waffles. The big backyard was safely fenced in and a great place for dogs, and people, to run around.

A moment later the front door opened and in walked Mrs. Benson. Taylor had been joking before but it really did feel like having two worlds collide to see our English teacher come into the shelter. She had changed out of her school clothes, a button-down shirt and khakis, and was now wearing jeans and a sweatshirt that said "Roxbury Park Softball League." The casual clothes just added to the weirdness of it.

Alice, who had gone into her office, popped back out to greet her.

"Hello and welcome," she said, reaching out to shake her hand. Alice, with her hair falling out of its usual ponytail and her big T-shirt with little black paw prints across it, was great at putting both people and dogs at ease. Which was good, because I realized that tough-as-nails Mrs. Benson actually looked nervous. And then I saw why. The little dog she was carrying was stiff as a board in her arms.

"This is Missy," Mrs. Benson said. The dog, who looked like a Yorkie with her pointed ears and long black and brown fur, burrowed her face into the side of Mrs. Benson's sweatshirt, as though she wanted to hide from all of us. And seeing how scared Missy was made me forget my own worries about my English teacher being here.

I walked up to them. "Hi, Mrs. Benson," I said.

"Hi, Kim," she said, smiling, which was a really rare thing to see. "You're a big part of the reason Missy and I are here."

"Really?" I asked, shocked.

Mrs. Benson nodded. "When you wrote about the shelter and starting up the Dog Club for your first English essay of the year, it sounded like such a great place for dogs. And then when I saw the pictures in *Our Roxbury Park* I knew for sure that this was the best place for Missy."

"We love dogs here," I said awkwardly. I wanted to pet Missy but I could tell she wasn't ready for that yet. "And they love coming in to play." Now I was just sounding stupid and I bit my lip.

But Mrs. Benson nodded. "Right, and I think that's wonderful for the dogs in your care," she said. "They need lots of love and attention. And even more than that I was really struck by your descriptions of the dogs, how sensitive you were to each of their needs."

"That's why we call her the dog whisperer," Taylor

26

said, coming over and slinging an arm around my neck. Chatty Taylor with her soft Southern accent could talk to anyone, and just having her next to me made me relax.

"Kim is quite gifted at working with dogs," Alice agreed.

Her words made me feel warm like I'd just cuddled up under a cozy comforter.

"It sounds like it," Mrs. Benson agreed. "And I think Missy is going to need your help."

I turned my attention back to Missy as Mrs. Benson set her gently on the ground. Missy's fur should have been thick but it was patchy and thin. I also saw what looked like a scab on her side. "Was she hurt?" I asked.

"She still has some sores from her time in the puppy mill," Mrs. Benson said with a sad sigh. "The vet gave me ointment and they're healing nicely. Her fur is growing back in and basically she's a healthy pup, at least physically."

I looked at Mrs. Benson, not exactly sure what she meant.

"It's her spirit that still needs some mending," Mrs. Benson explained. "She's skittish and shy and won't play with other dogs. Or people. That's why I was so happy when I found out about your club. It seems like a great way for Missy to learn how to play with other dogs and meet some new people who can show her true kindness."

I squatted near Missy, though not too close. Missy's whole body was rigid as she looked firmly away from everyone around her. She was small, which only added to how vulnerable she seemed. And in that moment I fell in love with her. "We'll take great care of her, Mrs. Benson," I said.

Mrs. Benson smiled again and this time I wasn't seeing her as my teacher. I was seeing her as the owner of a dog who needed help.

"I know you will," she said.

"We just need some information so Missy can join the club," Sasha said. She had come up behind me and was holding our client list as well as the Dog Club notebook where we recorded information about each dog. That's how we kept track of which dogs preferred not to be touched on their tails, what games they liked best, and all kinds of other things that helped us take the best possible care of all our clients. I knew Missy was going to have a long entry. A dog whose trust had been abused would be sensitive to all kinds of behaviors.

Mrs. Benson answered Sasha's questions while I kept an eye on Missy. She was like a dog statue, not moving a muscle or even her eyes. But I could see the sides of her little body moving rapidly, which meant she was breathing fast. And that meant she was anxious. The dogs still inside, Popsicle, Mr. S, Gus, and Gracie, all seemed to sense Missy's apprehension. Normally they all ran up to greet a newcomer but today they were all giving Missy space, which was clearly exactly what she needed.

"Okay, that's all the information we need for now," Sasha said in her businesslike way. We all took the Dog Club and our roles in it seriously. "You can check our blog after every meeting. It's called the Dog Club Diary and Kim writes up a report of what all the dogs did."

"And Taylor posts pictures," I added.

"I'll look forward to that," Mrs. Benson said.

"We also have a pickup service," Sasha said, explaining how we could get Missy and bring her to the shelter.

Mrs. Benson tipped her head, as though considering. "I hope in a few months Missy will be ready for that," she said after a moment. "But right now she isn't trained to be on a leash and I think it's better if I bring her in."

"Sure, that makes sense," Sasha said. "I think that covers everything. Welcome to the Roxbury Park Dog Club, Missy!"

I smiled at our newest member. It was going to take a lot of love and patience but I was confident that we could mend Missy's broken spirit.

3

"Is the table set?" my mom called from the kitchen where she was cooking up pumpkin soup for dinner. The spicy scent had my stomach rumbling and I poked my brother, Matt, who was supposed to be helping me by putting out plates but was leaning on the dining room table and sending a text instead.

"Hang on," Matt said, eyes glued to the screen of his phone.

Just then my stomach growled loudly.

Matt looked up and blinked. "What kind of monster is that?" he asked.

"A hungry one," I told him.

"I guess I better get on it," he said, laughing as he stuffed his phone into his pocket and took four plates from the cabinet along the wall. Our parents owned the Rox, a popular diner in town, so our kitchen cabinets were overflowing with ingredients and cooking utensils that my mom used to create new recipes. Two years ago we ran out of room for dishes in the kitchen, so my dad built a shelving unit in the dining room. It actually made setting the table a whole lot easier since the dishes and silverware were all right next to the big oak table where we ate.

"That smells so good," I said to Matt as I put out glasses for everyone.

"Fingers crossed," Matt said, grinning. My mom always tried out new recipes at home first. Most of her creations were pretty awesome but every once in a while there was a true food disaster, like the time she tried to make a salmon sweet potato casserole. But tonight I couldn't wait to dig in.

"Table's set," Matt called.

"Perfect timing," my dad said. He was acting as my mom's assistant chef. I'd heard them laughing as they chopped up pumpkin slices earlier. "Everything's ready."

With all four of us it didn't take long to bring all the food out, and a few minutes later we were digging into the thick soup along with slices of the crusty bread my dad had baked and a spinach salad.

"Mmm," I said. The soup was perfect—rich and creamy with just a hint of cinnamon.

"Kim called it," Matt said. He was practically halfway through his bowl already. My parents joked that Matt didn't eat his food, he inhaled it. "This is great."

"I'm glad you guys think so," my mom said. "We'll add it to our list of fall specials."

"You should have a pumpkin theme," Matt said. "Pumpkin pie, pumpkin cookies, pumpkin ice cream."

"That sounds like more of a dessert theme," my dad said, grinning as he spread butter on his bread.

"Oh, that's a great theme," I said, and Matt reached over to give me a high five.

"So give us the scoop from the day," my mom said to Matt and me.

Matt told us about the geometry test he'd aced and the story he was writing for the school paper. He was a sophomore at Roxbury High and unlike me he always got great grades without even trying. Which was part of the problem—my parents were used to Matt just gliding his way through school. I knew how much they wanted to help me but they didn't quite know what to do about a kid who tripped up more than she glided when it came to math tests and English papers.

But I didn't want to think about that now or I'd lose my appetite.

"How was your day, Kim?" my mom asked when Matt was done talking and had started slurping down his third bowl of soup.

"We had a surprise in Dog Club today," I said. "Our

new client is Mrs. Benson, my English teacher."

Matt almost choked on his soup. "Mrs. Benson has a dog?" he asked. He'd had Mrs. Benson when he was in seventh grade too and he knew how tough she was. "That is really hard to imagine. Dogs make people all goofy and warm. And that is so not Mrs. Benson."

"People have different sides," my dad said.

"Yeah, it was definitely like that today," I agreed. "A new side of Mrs. Benson."

"Does she talk to her dog in silly voices like you do?" Matt teased.

I scowled at him. "I do not use silly voices," I said loftily. "And neither does Mrs. Benson." As I remembered Missy my annoyance at my brother disappeared. "Actually she mostly just seemed worried about her dog, Missy. She's a rescue from a puppy mill."

Matt's joking grin evaporated. "Oh, that's tough," he said.

"Good for her for taking in a needy dog," my mom said sympathetically.

"Though do you think the Dog Club might

overwhelm a dog like that?" my dad asked. My parents knew about the problems we'd had in the past.

"It'll be hard for her at first," I said. "She was so scared today she barely even moved. But I think after a few visits she'll begin to get more comfortable."

"How sad," my mother said sympathetically. "I hope you guys can help her."

"Are you kidding?" Matt asked. "The dog whisperer here can help all dogs."

Matt may leave smelly socks around the house and annoy me with his teasing but in the end he always has my back. I smiled my thanks at him.

"Yes, Kim is certainly gifted with dogs," my dad said in a way that made it sound like he was saying something else. I glanced at him and noticed that he hadn't eaten very much. My mom either. And neither of them were asking me about school, which was weird—usually they wanted to hear all about what we were doing in math and English and even the classes where I was doing okay, like science and social studies. It must have been a busy day at the Rox.

"I've got to go start my geometry homework," Matt said. He did activities after school most days, so the evening was his homework time. "Just pile the dishes in the sink and I'll do them later." It was my night to clear the table and his to wash up. He headed upstairs, leaving my parents and me to finish eating.

"This soup really is good," I told my mom, serving myself just a little more and cutting half a slice of bread to go with it.

"Thanks, hon," she said. When she smiled I noticed the dark circles under her eyes. She was definitely tired after a long day at work. "And actually there's something Dad and I need to talk to you about."

"Is everything okay?" I asked, concerned something else was making her tired.

My mom exchanged a quick look with my dad. "We think it's good news."

The way she said it made it sound like she thought I might not agree.

"We know you've been struggling a lot in seventh grade," my dad said.

So this was about school. The bread I was chewing suddenly felt like a lump of raw dough in my mouth.

"And we know how hard you've been trying," my mom added, stirring her soup absently. "It's not your fault, but you've fallen behind and catching up is a challenge."

"I have been working hard and I'll work even harder," I promised once I'd managed to swallow the bread. "I know I can catch up."

My mom reached over and patted my hand. "We see how you're giving it your all, but Kim, we're starting to think that maybe Roxbury Middle School just isn't the right place for you. You're always stressed out about studying and we think you might be happier somewhere else."

"What?" I asked, shocked. Sure things were hard and I wasn't getting the best grades, but Roxbury Park Middle School was where my friends were and it was the reason we'd started the Dog Club. All of which meant Roxbury Park Middle School was the perfect place for me.

"Last week the Partridges came into the Rox," my dad said. "Remember them? They had a son a few years older than you, George."

I nodded since I vaguely remembered George, though I had no idea what he or his parents had to do with any of this.

"Well, George had some struggles at Roxbury Park Middle School too," my mom said, picking up the story. "And his parents enrolled him at Blue Orchard Academy."

"The private school?" I asked with a sinking feeling in my stomach. I suddenly wished I hadn't eaten so much soup.

"Yes, the one just over in Middletown," my dad said. Middletown was next to Roxbury Park, though we didn't go there often—everything we needed was right here in town.

"The Partridges said that George has just blossomed at Blue Orchard," my mom said cheerfully. "His grades went up, he started understanding everything in his classes—"

"He's made great friends," my dad interrupted enthusiastically. "And he even joined the school band."

"I have friends," I pointed out. The soup was starting to slosh around in my stomach. "And I don't play an instrument so I don't need a band."

"But you do need a school where you can learn and do well," my mom said softly. "Without so much struggle and stress."

"Blue Orchard has small classes," my dad said. "So you can get a lot of individual attention."

"That's probably what you need to raise your grades," my mom said. "And if it isn't, all the teachers have office hours to meet with students who need some extra help."

I was starting to worry I was about to throw up. The thought of leaving my school and my friends made me sick. "I love Roxbury Park Middle School," I said. My voice was shaky.

"We know that," my dad said. "But it's also the only school you know. We think if you give Blue Orchard a chance you'll see how much better it could be, how much happier you would be in a school where you can thrive."

This was awful. "I don't want to go to Blue Orchard," I said. Tears stung my eyes and the soup was a hurricane in my stomach.

"We understand," my dad said. "Change like this is always scary. And we're not saying a decision has been made."

I let out a deep breath at those words. No decision made was good, very good.

"We'd just like you to keep an open mind," my mom said. "We'll go for a tour and an interview, look around and then apply if it seems like it could be a good fit."

"We'd have to apply fast," my dad said. "So that you could start in January."

"Wait, in January?" I asked. "That's so soon."

"Right," my dad agreed, like that was a good thing.

"That's when their new semester begins," my mom explained. "So you wouldn't have to wait a whole year to enroll."

"But nothing's definite, right?" I asked, clinging to that.

My parents looked at each other before answering.

"We'll take it one step at a time," my dad said.

"But Kim," my mom said, her face serious as she leaned forward and took my hand. "This could be an amazing opportunity for you and we need to seriously consider it."

4

"Hey," Sasha called as I came up to the corner where she and Taylor were waiting for me the next morning. We always met up and walked to school together, something I was especially thankful for today.

"Is everything okay?" Taylor asked. It was a crisp fall day and she was wearing a bright blue hoodie with rhinestones on it. "You never texted last night."

We always texted each other at night, just checking

in and stuff. But last night I'd turned off my phone and put every bit of energy I had into my homework.

Sasha looked at me closely. "You're not okay," she said, worried. "What's wrong?"

The concern in her voice was all it took for tears to spring to my eyes. "My parents talked to me last night," I said, my voice wobbly. "About how I'm having trouble in school."

My friends waited while I took a breath. "They want me to apply to that private school, Blue Orchard."

Sasha gasped.

"And if I get in they want me to start in January," I finished.

Taylor's eyes were huge. "They can't be serious," she said.

As always it made me feel better to tell my friends.

"They are," I confirmed. "They think the smaller classes will help me catch up and get better grades."

"But you can't leave us," Sasha said plaintively.

As we started walking to school, a sudden gust of

wind rustled the leaves that were scattered on the side-walk.

"We have to stop this," Taylor said, her voice determined. "Have they sent in an application already?"

"They want me to fill it out this week," I said, remembering what my parents had told me last night. "And then they need some samples of my schoolwork before they can mail it in to Blue Orchard."

"Maybe we can sabotage the application," Taylor mused.

Sasha shook her head grimly. "That only works on TV," she said. "We need a real-world plan. We have to keep Kim at Roxbury Park Middle School with us, where she belongs."

"Right," Taylor said, nodding.

"We're not letting you go," Sasha said, squeezing my arm. "Not without a fight."

"And you know when we fight for something we get it," Taylor said. It was true. We'd had our share of struggles at the Dog Club, but after digging in and working hard, we'd always come out on top. This was different, but maybe if we put our heads together we *could* come up with a plan to keep me here. After all, if we'd managed to face down the Pampered Puppy and keep our business strong, we could probably do anything.

"Thanks, you guys," I said, smiling for the first time since I'd heard the name Blue Orchard.

"You can thank us with a party after we fix this problem," Taylor joked as we crossed Montgomery Street.

"If we can keep my parents from sending me away I'll throw the biggest party of the year," I said. We'd reached the path that led to the main doors of the school. Normally I barely even glanced at the big brick building but today I gazed up at it, appreciating how happy I was to be here. And how much I wanted to stay. "And last night I worked really hard on my homework. I think if I show my parents that I *can* get good grades here, they won't make me leave."

"That's a good start," Sasha said. "And we can help you. We can start at lunch."

"Bri is eating with us today," Taylor said regretfully. "I already invited her."

"Right," Sasha said. "That's okay. Kim probably did a great job on her homework." She turned back to me. "We can just help you study for the next tests you have."

"Okay, thanks," I said. I was still hoping that if I put in a little more time, I'd be able to fix this on my own. Though if I did need their help for a few weeks, just to catch up, it wasn't really that big of a deal.

We walked through the big double doors and into the hallway, which smelled like old sneakers and pine cleaner. For the first time I realized how much I liked that smell.

"We have a plan," Taylor said, slinging an arm over my shoulders as we joined the crowd walking toward the locker alcoves. "Which is good. Because you're not going anywhere and that's final."

I grinned. "Sounds great to me!"

"I brought something to share with everyone," Brianna said shyly. We were sitting at our usual lunch table along the back wall of the cafeteria with our friends Naomi, Emily, Rachel, and Dana at the table right next to us.

"You brought enough for us too, right?" Emily asked, leaning over with a grin.

"Of course," Brianna said, grinning back. "I know how this works."

She'd sat with us once before and seen that we often brought in extra treats to share. Food always tasted better when we all ate it all together.

"So what did you bring?" Taylor asked. She had her usual yogurt and granola in front of her but she was peering at the big Tupperware in Brianna's hands.

Brianna pried off the top. "Steamed sweet buns," she said, passing the container to Taylor. "My grandmother is from China and she taught me and my mom how to make them."

Taylor plucked one out. They were small and round and smelled sugary. "They're moist," Taylor said.

"I hope you guys like them," Brianna said, twisting

a lock of hair as we passed the buns around, everyone taking one.

"I'm sure we will," Taylor said.

I bit into mine. The bread was pleasantly chewy and inside was a thick, sweet, creamy filling.

"These are really good," Taylor said. "What's the filling made out of?"

"Bean paste," Brianna said, grinning. "I didn't want to tell you guys that part before you tried them because here beans aren't sweet. But in China they get creative with red beans and good things happen."

"Whatever they do is working," Naomi said. She'd finished hers already. "These are delish. Thanks, Brianna."

Rachel, Dana, and Emily echoed their thanks and then the four of them turned back to their lunches.

"I can't believe this is made with beans," Sasha said as she took her last bite. "It's so sweet."

"Kim, I bet your mom would love to try one," Taylor said. She'd finished hers and was taking the foil off her yogurt. "Kim's family owns the Rox and her mom is a total foodie," she explained to Brianna.

"Cool," Brianna said. "I love the Rox—especially the sweet potato fries you guys make."

"They're a house specialty," I said. Usually it made me proud to talk about the Rox, but today I didn't want to think about my parents because that would just make me think about Blue Orchard.

"So Bri, guess who our newest Dog Club client is?" Taylor asked.

It still felt a little weird to watch Taylor be nice to the person who had been so mean to her. I was definitely keeping an eye on Brianna, who just looked interested in what Taylor was saying.

"Who?" Brianna asked. She'd gotten a bowl of mac and cheese and a side of broccoli and was mixing them together. It looked and smelled delicious. I usually just got a turkey sandwich but something hot on a chilly day might taste really good. I decided I'd try it on the next cold, rainy day.

"Mrs. Benson," Taylor said.

Brianna's eyes widened. "You're kidding!"

"It's true," Taylor said, swirling her spoon around her yogurt. "She has a little tan and black dog—Kim, what kind of dog is Missy?"

"She's a Yorkie," I said. I had a big dog collage on my wall and I knew my breeds.

"Oh, with the little pointed ears and kind of square jaw?" Brianna asked me.

"Right," I said, starting in on the second half of my sandwich.

"They're so cute," Brianna said. A group of eighth-grade boys walked past and one of them almost hit her in the head with his lunch tray. "Watch it," Brianna said sharply. I hadn't liked it when she used that tone with Taylor but it was cool how she stood up for herself. I just felt shy around the eighth graders, especially the boys.

"Missy is cute," I agreed. "But she's also really timid. Mrs. Benson adopted her from a puppy mill rescue."

Everyone else had looked sad at this news but Bri-anna's mouth pressed into a thin line and her eyes darkened. She wasn't just sad about this—she was mad. "Those places infuriate me," she said angrily. "They have no right to mistreat innocent animals."

"I know," I agreed, instantly liking Brianna a little more. "Puppy mills are awful."

"I'm glad Mrs. Benson took one of those dogs in," Brianna said. "They need loving homes." Then her brows crinkled together. "How will you guys work with Missy in Dog Club? Won't she attack the other dogs?"

"No," I said. I'd read enough about dogs rescued from puppy mills to know that the opposite was true. "They generally aren't aggressive at all. The challenge is that they're scared of everything. They've retreated into themselves and you have to work really hard to win their trust." I remember how Mrs. Benson had put it. "It's like the experience of living in those little cages breaks their spirits, so you have to help build them back up."

Brianna tilted her head thoughtfully. "I guess that makes sense," she said. "But it sounds tough."

I thought of Missy and how rigidly she had stood at the shelter yesterday, ignoring everyone and everything around her. It was like she had tried to be invisible. "It'll take time," I said. "Lots of baby steps to help bring her out of her shell."

Brianna nodded. "I can see why Taylor says you're the dog whisperer," she said, a note of admiration in her voice.

"Taylor says that because she's a good friend," I said, shooting Taylor a grin.

"I'm just a big-hearted Southern girl," Taylor said in a drawl that made us all laugh. "But honestly, Kim is amazing with dogs. You should come see for yourself sometime."

Sasha and I looked at each other, not sure that was such a great idea. Sitting with us at lunch was one thing, but the shelter was *our* place, just the three of us. Plus not so long ago Brianna's mom was attacking our Dog Club as unprofessional. Yes, that was in the past now, but I wasn't sure I was ready to welcome Brianna to our club. And I could tell from Sasha's raised eyebrow that she was thinking the exact same thing.

But Brianna was nodding enthusiastically. "I'd love to visit your Dog Club," she said happily. "It sounds like you guys have so much fun there. The Pampered Puppy is nice and all but we're so busy training the dogs we barely play. Plus they have to stay clean for their owners."

I thought of the afternoon two weeks ago when we'd played outside after a rainstorm and all the dogs got covered in mud. We'd hosed them off as best we could but they all still had a few muddy patches when they went home, and none of the owners had minded at all. This was why it was good that Roxbury Park had two dog-care options. At least it was good as long as both places were nice about it. And in fairness it did seem like Brianna was excited to see our club.

"Don't you have your volunteer job after school?" Sasha asked Brianna. She had finished her salad and was eating the packet of crackers she'd gotten with it.

"Yeah, at the library," Brianna said, wrinkling her nose. "There are too many of us there, so there's never anything to do. Most of us just sit around doing homework until it's time to go home."

"That's too bad," Taylor said, her brows knitting together in concern. "The volunteer project is my favorite part of school."

"Yeah, because you have a great project," Brianna said wistfully.

"Well it sounds like you can miss a day at the library," Taylor said. "So you should come to our next Dog Club."

Brianna smiled but before accepting she turned to Sasha and me. "Is that okay with you guys?"

It was nice that she asked. And even though I still had my doubts, there was no way that I could refuse, not when she was so eager. Plus, it would just be the one time, and we could handle anything once.

Sasha and I glanced at each other quickly and I knew she felt the same. "Sure," Sasha said as the bell rang and we began gathering up our stuff. "It'll be fun."

I just hoped she was right.

5

Hattie and I were the first to arrive at our next Dog Club meeting. It was a gray day with a misty rain, so I grabbed a towel to dry Hattie's fluffy fur before setting her loose to greet her friends. A moment later Tim and Caley walked in.

"Hey, Kim," Caley said with a smile. Her red hair was held back in a sloppy bun secured with two pens and she wore a pair of worn-out overalls over a bright pink thermal shirt. On someone else it might have looked silly but Caley made everything she wore look good. I secretly hoped to be like her when I was in high school.

"What's up?" Tim said as Boxer ran over and jumped up on him. "Oof," Tim gasped. "Hang on there, big guy. We'll play as soon as I hang up my coat." Tim's black hair was wet from the mist outside and he shook his head, spraying drops on Caley like a puppy after a bath.

"Hey!" Caley squealed. "It's your business if you don't carry an umbrella, but don't soak the rest of us."

"Umbrellas are for wimps," Tim said, heading over to the bins of toys where he searched out Boxer's favorite green Frisbee, a chewed up mess that no one would ever throw out because Boxer loved it so much.

"Dry wimps," Caley retorted, rolling her eyes. But she was grinning.

Lily and Daisy went to join Tim and Boxer for a game of Frisbee while Hattie and Gracie began a spirited session of tug-of-war. Waffles came over to snuggle with me. I'd just settled on the floor with him when the door opened and Sasha came in with Mr. S, Popsicle, and Humphrey.

"It's starting to come down out there," Sasha said as she picked up the towel to dry off all three dogs. It was hard because they were bouncing around, ready to play.

I went over to help her.

"Hey, Mr. S," I said, reaching down to pat Sasha's dog. He wagged his tail joyfully as I wiped him down. Humphrey collapsed at my feet and let me dry him off. Then he got up to join Waffles, who was playing with a red rubber ball.

"So are they here yet?" Sasha asked me.

"No," I said. "It's going to be interesting to see what Brianna thinks of the shelter."

"We have guests coming?" Tim asked. He was already panting from running around with Boxer and Lily.

"Taylor's friend Brianna is coming today," I said.

"Cool," Tim said, grabbing the Frisbee and tossing

it one way while he ran the other. Lily chased after him while Boxer raced for the toy.

Caley was now throwing the ball for Humphrey and Waffles but she looked over at me and Sasha. "Taylor's friend but not yours?" she asked quizzically. Nothing escaped Caley.

"Um, we're not sure yet," Sasha said.

"As long as she's nice to Taylor we're okay with her," I added.

Caley nodded. "Same goes for me," she said. "Dog Club members have to stick together."

Her words gave me a warm feeling.

"Hey, everyone," Alice said, poking her head out of her office. Today she was wearing my favorite of her dog shirts, the one that said "Roxbury Park Dog Club."

"We match," Sasha said happily. She and I had both worn our club shirts that day. I loved wearing mine and showing the world how proud I felt about our club.

"Me too," Tim said, peeling off his gray sweatshirt to reveal his Dog Club T-shirt. "Great minds think alike," he said to Caley, who pretended to pout.

"Next time send me the wardrobe memo, guys," she said.

Just then the door opened and Taylor came in, Brianna right behind her. They were laughing as they unleashed Coco and Gus.

"Hey, everybody," Taylor said. Her eyes were sparkling: clearly she was having a good time. I felt myself warming to Brianna just a bit more.

But then I noticed how Brianna's nose was slightly wrinkled as she looked around the shelter. I followed her gaze. We'd just gotten a new floor but it was already scuffed from doggy paws running around all day. The paint on the walls was a bit faded and there were toys strewn all about. I remembered the pictures of the Pampered Puppy from their website: everything there was sleek and polished to a shine.

"Um, what's this?" Brianna asked, slightly horrified as Boxer carefully set his Frisbee at her feet.

"His favorite toy," I said indignantly. Boxer adored

his Frisbee and Brianna should have been honored to have him share it with her.

I glanced at Sasha and saw that she was frowning.

But then Brianna picked up the Frisbee and gave it a powerful toss across the room. Boxer barked happily and zoomed after it. "Well, if it's his favorite then we'll play with it," Brianna said. I noticed her fingers were wet from holding the drooly dog toy but she didn't seem worried about it. My annoyance at her melted away. Honestly, Boxer's Frisbee *was* kind of gross, especially if you weren't used to it.

Taylor introduced Brianna to Tim, Caley, and Alice while Sasha got out the laundry basket for a game of doggy basketball. I was about to join her when Mrs. Benson and Missy came in.

"Hello," Mrs. Benson said. Missy was in her arms but she was stiff as a board.

"Hi," I said, feeling a bit shy as I walked over to my teacher, who was wearing jeans and a bulky fleece jacket. It was still strange to see her outside the classroom in such casual clothes.

"Missy's ready for her first day of Dog Club," Mrs. Benson said. Her voice was cheery but I saw the way her forehead was creased and the concerned look she was giving her dog.

And just like that she wasn't my intimidating English teacher: she was a worried dog owner. And that was someone I could talk to.

"Hi, Missy," I said softly as Mrs. Benson set the little dog down. "We're glad you're here. No one's going to rush you. You just take your time getting comfortable."

Missy backed up so that she was tucked into the corner of the room, facing out. Then she remained frozen, but I saw her ears shift toward me the tiniest bit. She was listening.

"She likes you," Mrs. Benson said.

"I like her too," I said, looking affectionately at the scared pup. "She's going to do just fine here."

"Thanks, Kim," Mrs. Benson said warmly. "I know this is going to be a great experience for Missy. I suspect we'll both learn some things from her time here."

It was crazy to imagine that my teacher could learn anything from me. But a new dog owner could.

"Tell me about Missy," I said. I was standing close enough to Missy so that she could get used to the sound of my voice, but far enough away that she wouldn't feel threatened. "Just anything you think we should know about what she likes or doesn't like."

Mrs. Benson thought for a moment. "Well, she doesn't like it when people touch the back of her neck," she said.

"Oh, that must be because that's how she was picked up at the puppy mill," I said, remembering some of what I'd read. "She probably got grabbed roughly so it's a sensitive spot now."

"You've done some research," Mrs. Benson said approvingly. "That's just it. And she also doesn't like it when anyone gets behind her, though I'm not sure why that is."

"It's a trust issue," I said immediately. "Dogs only

let people or other dogs get behind them when they feel safe and secure."

"That explains it," Mrs. Benson said. Her mouth turned down sadly. "Poor Missy doesn't trust anyone."

"She'll learn to," I said. "It just takes time. And we have all the time in the world to let her get comfortable being here."

"Wonderful," Mrs. Benson said, smiling at me. The crease on her forehead was gone. "I'll be back to get her at pickup."

"See you then," I said, my attention already focused on Missy as Mrs. Benson waved to everyone and headed out. Dogs zoomed by and the air was filled with the sounds of happy barking and people laughing. Plus there were about a million unfamiliar smells: it was a lot for any dog the first time they came to Dog Club. And for a dog like Missy, it was probably totally overwhelming. I wished some of the dogs could go out back but the weather was too yucky.

"So this is Missy," Brianna said, coming over and

speaking quietly, which I appreciated. "She looks so scared."

"It's going to take some time for her to feel comfortable here," I said.

Brianna nodded. "That makes sense." Then she grinned. "But what I really can't believe is that Mrs. Benson owns jeans."

"Tell me about it," Taylor said, walking over to us. "When she came in the first time I thought I was seeing things."

I laughed at that, though I tried not to be too loud. I didn't want to startle Missy.

"So what's the plan?" Sasha asked me, her eyes sympathetic as she gazed down at Missy.

I looked around to take stock of things. Tim and Caley had the game of doggy basketball started and most of the dogs were playing. Tim had set the basket on the opposite side of the room so most of the action was far away from Missy, who was still in her corner.

"I think we should just let Missy stay here," I said.

"Should we try to pet her or anything?" Sasha asked uncertainly.

"No," I said, shaking my head. "Right now she needs us to give her some space."

"How do you know that?" Brianna asked.

"I'm not sure exactly," I said, trying to figure out how to explain what gave me that feeling, the one that always told me what a dog really needed. "Part of it is how she's standing," I said. "And the look in her eyes. The way she holds her ears too. But it's more than just looking at her—it's the feeling coming from her, if that makes sense."

"None at all," Taylor said cheerfully. "That's dog-whisperer talk."

I laughed, but Brianna was looking at me thoughtfully. "You really are good with dogs," she said. "We have trainers at the Pampered Puppy who've worked with dogs for years but don't get them the way you do."

"Thanks," I said, ducking my head. I hadn't expected her to say something so nice.

"Kim knows dogs," Sasha said proudly.

"So what will you do to help her feel safe?" Brianna asked, brushing a loose lock of hair out of her face.

"I'll talk to her, get her used to my voice," I said, hoping Brianna wouldn't think talking to dogs was weird. But she just nodded like that made sense. "And I'll make sure no balls hit her. Or Boxer's Frisbee."

"We can keep the other dogs from coming too close," Sasha said. "So Missy can have her own space."

"That would be great," I said.

"All right," Taylor said, rubbing her hands together. "Let's go take over this game of doggy basketball!"

The three of them headed off and I sat down about two feet away from Missy. Her gaze stayed glued to the spot in front her but her ears moved slightly as I moved. I leaned against the wall, my legs out in front of me to block any toys from rolling into Missy. Across the room Tim and Taylor were cheering on Boxer, who was racing toward the basket, ball in his mouth. But at the last minute Lily cut him off. She had his Frisbee in her mouth and the second Boxer saw that, he dropped the ball and took off after Lily.

"Boxer, you don't drop the ball on a big play!" Tim shouted.

"Way to go, Lily!" Caley, coach of the other team, cheered. "She's our secret weapon."

Taylor was doubled over laughing.

Sasha scooped up the ball and tossed it to Hattie, who ran toward the basket.

"That's Hattie with the ball," I told Missy, my voice pitched low and soothing. "She used to live here and she was shy just like you."

Missy didn't move and I wasn't sure if this was working. But I went on anyway.

"But she saw how nice the other dogs are," I said. "And how much we all loved her. And look how happy she is now." Hattie was flying joyfully across the room, ears streaming behind, Gracie right beside her.

When I looked back at Missy I saw one of her ears twitch. She was listening! I went on talking, telling her about the other dogs and about the Dog Club. Sure my brother, Matt, thought it was crazy to talk to dogs, but that was because he had never done it. Dogs were actually excellent listeners, way better than people a lot of the time. And as I talked I saw that Missy was relaxing the littlest bit. Her legs weren't quite so rigid and her tail even moved a few times. Just a little, but still, it was progress.

Brianna was now serving as the ref for a second game of basketball, the rematch Tim had demanded after his team lost the first one. Tim was a sore loser, something we all liked to tease him about. Brianna was doing a good job making calls and helping the dogs when they lost the game ball and tried to put other things in the basket.

But when she reached down to grab a rawhide dog bone that had somehow gotten into the fray, Mr. S crashed into her elbow, hard.

"Hey, what's wrong with this dog?" Brianna asked.

Taylor opened her mouth to try to stop what was

about to happen, but it was too late. No one insulted Mr. S and got away with it.

Sasha's glare was fierce. "Nothing's wrong with my dog," she snapped. "He's perfect! And he's nearly blind, so the fact that he gets around so well makes him extra amazing."

Brianna raised an eyebrow. "Relax," she said. "I didn't know."

It wasn't much of an apology and I could see Sasha's back was still stiff. Taylor looked anxiously between Brianna and Sasha, but then Lily and Boxer nearly ran into her as they headed for the basket.

"Taylor, help," Caley called, laughing at Tim, who was trying to get Gus to block Lily's shot. They hadn't heard what had happened between Sasha and Brianna.

Taylor cast a worried glance toward Sasha but then headed over to the game, Brianna right behind her.

"I can't believe she insulted Mr. S," Sasha grumbled, coming over and sitting with me and Missy, though on my other side so Missy wouldn't get spooked. She pulled Mr. S onto her lap and hugged him tight.

"You're like one of those mama bears that get all ferocious when something threatens one of its cubs," I told Sasha, still using my soothing voice for Missy, who had tensed up slightly when Sasha and Mr. S joined us. "But I don't blame you. Mr. S is perfect."

"And I don't like people putting him down," she said.

I reached over to pat sweet Mr. S. "Me neither," I said. "I think Brianna is used to the way things are at the Pampered Puppy."

"That's definitely where she belongs," Sasha said with a sniff. "I'm glad she'll be going back there after today."

While I did like Brianna's fiery side when it came to things like telling off eighth-grade boys and her attitude about things like puppy mills, I wasn't comfortable with the way she'd been so quick to judge Mr. S. It was nice that Taylor had invited her to see our club but it did seem like Brianna was a better fit at the sleeker doggy day care in town.

Just then Popsicle darted by with Boxer's Frisbee in his mouth. Boxer was bearing down on him and both dogs' nails were digging into the floor. Popsicle crashed into the laundry basket, which knocked Tim off balance. He grabbed onto Caley but instead of keeping him upright, they both fell into a heap. Popsicle, Daisy, and Boxer jumped happily on top of them, which made Caley shriek and Tim laugh so hard I worried he'd pull a muscle.

Sasha and Mr. S got up to rejoin the others while I turned my attention back to Missy. "There's a lot of excitement here," I told her. "And you might not believe it right now but one of these days you're going to love it. And you're going to be right in there, playing with the other dogs and scoring points in doggy basketball."

Missy's tail wagged, a real wag. It was all I could do to stop myself from leaning over to hug her. She wasn't ready, but she would be, just like she'd be ready to play one day.

I was sure of it.

6

"Let's get this ice cream in the freezer," my mom said cheerfully as we set the bags from Old Farm Market on the counter. We'd just gone grocery shopping and picked up supplies for tonight's sleepover at my house. That meant lots of snacks, ingredients for my mom's famous pasta sauce for dinner and my dad's secret recipe French toast for breakfast, and most importantly, fixings for milk shakes, a sleepover tradition. Normally I would practically be dancing around the kitchen as we put everything away. But this morning my parents had told me the latest about my application to Blue Orchard and the news was not good.

"Can you put the rest of this stuff away?" my mom asked. "I want to get started on the sauce."

"Sure," I said. My whole body felt heavy as I put bread and eggs in the fridge.

Just as I finished, the doorbell rang. As I padded up to the door in my dog paw slippers I could hear Sasha and Taylor laughing outside. I was glad they were here but at the same time I was dreading telling them about Blue Orchard.

"Happy sleepover!" Taylor cried when I opened the door.

"Come on in," I said, pushing aside the thoughts of Blue Orchard. There'd be time to talk about it after dinner. "Let's put your stuff away."

I led my friends upstairs to my room with its puppy posters on the wall and my china dog collection on the bookcase. My favorite part of my room was the collage on my closet door. It had all kinds of dog pictures and stickers plus bits of information about dogs and a paw print border that Sasha had made last summer. And of course all the latest photos were of club dogs, taken by our official club photographer, Taylor.

"You put up that shot I took of Waffles and Coco," Taylor said, going over to look at it after she'd set down her overnight bag.

Sasha laughed. "That sounds like a breakfast order—cocoa and waffles." She stepped around the two air mattresses on the floor to get a better look. "That is a great picture," she said.

Waffles and Coco were both at the laundry basket, on opposite sides. Their paws were up on the basket and their noses were just touching.

"It would be a perfect Valentine's Day card," I said.

"Thanks, guys," Taylor said. "And listen, I'm sorry about what Brianna said about Mr. S." She was looking at Sasha, who scowled.

"It's not your fault she was rude," Sasha said.

"I don't think she meant it, not really," Taylor said.

Sasha glanced at me, frowning, and I could tell she was thinking the same thing I was: Why was Taylor so quick to defend Brianna?

"You know I adore Mr. S," Taylor went on. "And I know Bri will too, if she gets to know him. She's just one of those people who has a loud bark."

"Or barks before they think," Sasha muttered.

Taylor laughed. "Yeah, that's it—she reacts before she thinks things through," she said. "But give her a chance and you'll see she's really a softie underneath."

I wasn't so sure about that and I could tell by the way Sasha was biting her lip that she wasn't convinced either. But Taylor was looking at us pleadingly, so we both nodded.

"Thanks," Taylor said. "I'm glad I gave her a second chance and I know you guys will be too."

I had some doubts, but I wanted to try for Taylor since it clearly meant so much to her.

It was dinnertime, so we headed back downstairs to set the table. The scent of my mom's rich tomato sauce perfumed the air and I realized I was starving.

"That smells so good," Taylor said, pulling plates down from the shelves. We all spent so much time at each other's houses that we knew where everything was.

"Your mom is such a good cook," Sasha said. She was setting out silverware.

"Thank you," my mom called from the kitchen. Our house was pretty small, so it wasn't far.

A few minutes later we were all seated at the table passing around a steaming serving bowl of spaghetti and a big salad. My dad opened the foil containing the garlic bread he'd made and gave us each a perfectly toasted slice.

"I think this sauce gets better every time you make it," Sasha said to my mom after we'd started eating.

"Thanks," my mom said. "I'm always making small changes to it. Tonight I used a little extra basil."

"Don't change it too much," Matt said. He was already nearly done with his and had a smear of sauce on his chin.

"Save some room for dessert," my dad said, looking slightly alarmed at how fast Matt was going. "We brought home a strawberry shortcake from the Rox."

"I always have room for cake," Matt said, reaching across the table for more spaghetti.

"I have this theory that we actually all have two stomachs," Taylor said. "One for regular food and one for dessert. So no matter how much dinner you eat, you always have room for something sweet."

Matt nodded approvingly. "I like that," he said. "I think you're onto something."

Taylor grinned as she twined spaghetti around her fork.

"So how's the Dog Club, girls?" my mom asked.

"Really good," Sasha said. "I got two emails from potential clients this morning."

"Sounds like business is great," my dad said. He was

dipping his garlic bread into some extra sauce on his plate.

"It really is, thanks to *Our Roxbury Park*," Sasha agreed. "People have been contacting us ever since the article came out."

"Those photos were beautiful," my mom said with a smile for Taylor, who beamed. Taylor's mom had died when she was young and while her dad and three older sisters took great care of her, I knew she liked these mom moments with my mom and Sasha's.

"How's Mrs. Benson's dog?" Matt asked.

"Still pretty timid," I said, thinking of sweet Missy as I took a bite of spaghetti.

"She just stands by herself, all tense," Sasha said. "I've never seen a dog act like that."

"Puppy mills can be brutal places," my mom said sadly.

"I don't understand how people can be so cruel to dogs," Taylor said.

"People will do some awful things to make money,"

Matt said. Now he had bread crumbs spilling down his shirt.

"How are you helping this dog?" my dad asked.

"Her name's Missy," Sasha told him. She smiled at me. "We're letting the resident dog whisperer work her magic."

My dad smiled at that. "So what tricks do you have up your sleeve this time?" he asked me.

"I think the key is taking it really slowly," I said, frowning as my mom served me some salad. I had been hoping she wouldn't notice that I'd skipped it. "Missy has issues with not being able to trust anyone. And when she lived in a cage, the only times she was touched she was grabbed roughly and it hurt. So we won't touch her until she lets us know she's ready."

"Does she tell you all this in your dog conversations?" Matt teased. "Or does she send you a text?"

I rolled my eyes. "Yes, because Mrs. Benson bought her dog a phone."

We all laughed at that.

"Seriously, how will you know when Missy is ready to be touched?" Matt asked. He was done with his three servings and he had his elbows propped on the table as he waited for the rest of us to finish so we could have dessert.

"She'll give us signs like coming up to us or leaning against us," I said. "She'll wag her tail, stuff like that." It would be more than that—I knew I'd be able to sense when Missy was ready—but I didn't want to say that to Matt because he'd just start teasing me again.

"How do you help gain her trust?" my mom asked.

"Kim's been talking to Missy," Sasha said, and then she shot a look at Matt. "Which is really smart because if Missy gets comfortable with Kim's voice then Kim becomes a safe person for her."

Matt and my parents nodded.

"We're also keeping the other dogs away from Missy for a bit," Taylor added, helping herself to more garlic bread. "So Missy doesn't get overwhelmed. It's funny— the dogs seem to know that Missy needs space. I haven't seen any of them try to get too close to her."

"They must pick up on her signals the same way Kim does," Sasha said.

"That all sounds good," my mom said.

"There might be more we can do too," I said. "I'm going to do some more research on puppy mill dogs to find out."

"Sounds good," Matt said, standing up and starting to clear the table. "Almost as good as that strawberry shortcake. Let's clean this up so we can get to it!"

After we'd had our cake and helped my parents clean up, we went into the kitchen to make our milk shakes. We started with our favorite ice-cream flavors—mine was mint chocolate chip, Taylor's was strawberry, and Sasha had recently fallen in love with coffee. What made our milk shakes really good, though, were the add-ins. Today we had toffee, rainbow sprinkles, Oreos, M&M's, and candied peanuts. And of course there was whipped cream to go on top.

"I need more Oreos," Sasha said, looking at her milk shake with a critical eye.

Taylor passed her the package. "I think I'm ready," she said, sticking the hand mixer into her glass. We watched as her ice cream, milk, and mix-ins whooshed up into a spiral. A minute later she was done.

I passed her the M&M's—we'd learned that those were best stirred in last—and she gave me the mixer. A few minutes later we each had an icy glass of thick shake covered with whipped cream.

My parents didn't let me eat in my room, so we headed to the small den next to the kitchen. My slippers scuffed softly on the tan rug that had worn patches from Matt playing hours of Wii games on the big TV on the back wall. There was an old and comfy denim sofa and matching armchair, plus a big coffee table. Sasha and I settled on the couch while Taylor perched in the chair. Matt and my parents were upstairs, so it almost felt like we had the whole house to ourselves.

"I think I might have overdone it on the Oreos,"

Sasha said after trying to drink her shake. "I can't even get this out of the glass."

This happened a lot and I passed her the spoon I'd brought in so she could scoop it out.

"Thanks," she said. Then her forehead wrinkled just slightly. "Kim, is there something wrong? You're not drinking your shake."

There was no hiding anything from my friends.

"Kind of," I said, sinking back into the sofa with a sigh. "My parents had me finish up the application to Blue Orchard and they sent it in yesterday. Express mail."

"Oh no," Taylor cried while Sasha nearly choked on her shake.

"That was so fast," Sasha said when she recovered.

"Yeah," I agreed. "They're really excited about it." Thinking about it had killed my appetite, so I set my half-full shake on the coffee table. "Like they went to school this week to pick up samples of my work from my teachers. So they wouldn't have to wait for them to come in the mail."

Sasha grimaced. "Yikes, they really are into this idea."

"I know," I said glumly. "They gave me about a hundred Blue Orchard brochures to try to get me to want to go there."

"But it didn't work, right?" Taylor asked.

I shook my head so hard my hair whipped against my cheeks. "No way," I said. "It made me want to go even less because I found out something awful."

My friends waited, their faces tense.

"Blue Orchard doesn't let out until four every day," I said.

Sasha's face turned pale. "You wouldn't be able to come to Dog Club," she gasped.

"Right," I said, the word scratchy in my throat. "The drive from Middletown is almost half an hour with no stops. So by the time the bus got me home it would be after five."

"Kim, this is awful," Taylor said, her eyes wide.

None of us were drinking our shakes, and the ice cream was melting. I stared at the wet rings forming on the plastic top of the table and blinked back tears. "If I have to go to school there I'll lose everything," I said, my voice breaking.

My friends were instantly next to me, each with an arm tight around my shoulders.

"We are not letting that happen," Sasha said firmly.

"No way you're going anywhere," Taylor agreed.

"I'm not sure there's anything I can do to convince my parents to let me stay," I said. "They seem sure that I'll get in, and if I do I think that's it."

"Okay, it's time to step up the plan," Taylor said, an edge of steel in her soft Southern accent as she leaned forward. "We're going to show your parents that you belong with us, at Roxbury Park Middle School."

"But how?" I asked.

"I've been thinking about it," Taylor said, suddenly looking a tiny bit sheepish. "Actually more than thinking about it. I know we talked about me and Sash helping you study, but last night I didn't understand the math homework and Anna showed me how to do it." Anna was one of Taylor's older sisters. They hadn't always gotten along but lately they'd come to a good understanding and were really there for each other. Anna also happened to be a math genius. "She loves math and she's super good at explaining stuff—way better than Mr. Russo. And so I asked if she'd be willing to tutor you and she said she would."

Before I could fully process this, Sasha spoke up. "I've been doing more than thinking too," she admitted. "I asked Caley if she'd be willing to tutor you in English, since it's her favorite subject and all, and she said yes."

Now both my friends were looking at me eagerly. I really didn't want any tutors. I had to be able to do this stuff myself. Needing help gave me a squirmy feeling, like there really was something wrong with me.

But then I thought about having to leave Dog Club because I hadn't managed to get my grades up high enough. This was an emergency and emergencies called for serious action. It would just be a few weeks, to help me catch up and show my parents that I didn't need Blue Orchard's small classes or extra teacher time to get good grades. So I smiled at my friends. "That sounds great," I said. "Thanks so much, you guys."

Sasha grinned. "I think this will work," she said. "We have three weeks until our next big English test. That's plenty of time for Caley to teach you everything you could ever need to know about *Tom Sawyer*."

"And Anna will have you ready for our weekly math tests in no time at all," Taylor said, her sisterly pride shining through.

"And we'll help too," Sasha said. "We can quiz you and stuff."

Her words gave me that squirmy feeling again, but I stifled it. Right now I was in crisis mode and I needed to do everything I could to keep from being sent to Blue Orchard. "Thanks," I said, grinning at my friends. They really were the best.

"Now, we better finish these before they turn into ice-cream puddles," Taylor joked, picking up her glass.

"To Kim staying at Roxbury Park Middle School," Sasha said, raising her glass for a toast.

"Hear, hear!" Taylor chimed in as the three of us clinked our glasses together.

7

"Did you guys see all the comments on our latest Dog Club Diary blog post?" Sasha asked as we headed toward the shelter after school. The sun was bright and felt warm on my face as we walked. "There must have been twenty at least."

"Awesome," Taylor said as she crunched through a pile of leaves on the sidewalk.

"A lot of them liked that picture of Mr. S and Humphrey," I said. The two had been sleeping curled up together in a little furry pile and Taylor had given it the caption "Tuckered out." Our parents didn't want us posting any shots of us, since the Dog Club Diary was a public site, so all the photos were of dogs only.

"People had good stuff to say about the blog too," Taylor said, shooting me a grin. I'd had fun writing up a description of the latest game of doggy basketball. Somehow writing about the dogs was pleasure while the short essay I'd had to write for English last night was pure torture. It would be kind of a relief to get some help from Caley today.

"It's great that we have so many followers," Sasha said. "But a lot of them want to sign their dogs up for the club and I think we need to take a break from new dogs since we just brought in Missy."

I nodded as we waved to our neighbor Mr. Matsui, who was driving by in his truck. He ran a local construction crew and he'd been a big help a few years ago when my parents remodeled the Rox. "That's a good point," I said. "It's a big deal for all the dogs when a new one joins the club. We don't want to rock the boat too much."

"Right," Sasha said. "But what do we tell these people who want to get in?"

"That's kind of a problem," I said. Then I grinned. "A really good problem though."

"Totally," Sasha agreed, smiling.

"I think we start a wait list," Taylor said, twirling one of her braids between her fingers. She'd recently gotten new beads in, blue, pink, and silver, and they looked good with her bright pink sweater.

"That's a smart idea," I said. We were almost at the corner of Market and Grove, where we'd split up to get our dogs. Today I was picking up Coco and Gus.

"It is," Sasha agreed. "I'll set it up and then start taking names."

"Sounds good," Taylor said. "See you guys at the shelter."

We waved to each other and then headed off to get our dogs.

★ ★ ★

"What a pretty new collar you have," I told Missy. We were settled into what I now thought of as our usual spots, Missy standing stiff as a board in the front corner of the room and me sitting a few feet away. "That gold looks perfect on you."

Missy didn't look at me but I saw her ears twitch. Not surprisingly—after all, everyone loved a compliment. "Your fur is growing in so nicely," I went on in my calm voice. Her coat really was starting to look healthier. The patches were filling in and the scabs were fading. Soon Missy would look like any other Yorkie, though she would still have scars hidden on the inside. Scars that I was sure the club could help heal.

"Since it's nice out Tim and Caley took Boxer, Coco, and Lily to play in the backyard," I told Missy. "You remember them I bet. One of these days you'll be ready to go to the yard, too, and I think you'll really like it there." I shifted slightly as I continued. "See how Hattie, Waffles, Daisy, and Mr. S are playing fetch with

Taylor?" I asked. "That looks fun. And I think Gus and Gracie are having a grand old time with Sasha playing tug-of-war with that plastic bone." I'd started telling Missy the names of the dogs and people in the club so that they'd become familiar to her.

Just then Humphrey came over to me, a tennis ball in his mouth. Popsicle was right behind him. Humphrey dropped the ball, which rolled gently into my hand, and both dogs looked at me eagerly.

"Humphrey and Popsicle want to play fetch," I told Missy, getting to my feet, careful not to make any sudden moves and startle her. "You can come with us or just watch if you want." I felt a little bad leaving her, but the other dogs needed me too. Plus it was probably good for Missy to have a bit of alone time. I walked toward the side of the room, away from where the others were playing, and tossed the ball for Humphrey and Popsicle, who both ran after it.

"Kim," Sasha called. Her eyes were bright and she pointed to something behind me. I turned to look and felt a tug in my chest. Missy had come with us. Her back was still to the wall and her legs were still stiff, but she wanted to stay close to me.

"That's amazing," Taylor said.

I grinned. "It's a good first step," I said.

Missy stayed close as I played with the other dogs and I was careful to keep the ball away from her. Being run down by Humphrey and Popsicle, small though they were, was not what Missy needed right now.

"Hey, check out Missy," Caley said when she came in a few minutes later. "Looks like the dog whisperer is having an effect already."

I couldn't help grinning at that.

Caley hung her coat up and then came over to me. "So I hear you want to talk *Tom Sawyer* with me," she said in her friendly way.

I'd been worried it would feel awkward to have Caley tutor me at the shelter, but it turned out the opposite was true. Being surrounded by dogs and having Missy nearby made me feel like it was no big deal.

"That'd be great," I said.

Caley took a turn tossing the tennis ball. "Okay, so where are you guys in the book?"

Caley and I spent the next half hour talking about *Tom Sawyer* and playing fetch with Popsicle, Daisy, and Waffles after Humphrey got tired and headed to a sunny spot near the front window for a nap. Oscar, the shelter cat who thought he was a dog, was curled up on the windowsill above him, making it look like they were in bunk beds. Taylor got a picture that I was sure would be perfect for the blog.

". . . which is the theme in the first part of the book," Caley finished as Tim, Lily, Coco, and Boxer came in from the backyard.

"Thanks," I told her. "I feel like I'm starting to understand it better."

"Great," Caley said as Boxer came over to greet us. "We can talk again after you guys read more."

I wasn't positive that everything we'd talked about was the kind of stuff Mrs. Benson was going to ask us about on the next test, but I did feel like I got the first few chapters of the story better. And that had to be a good thing.

We spent the rest of the afternoon playing dog tag, and too soon owners started to arrive. Hattie ran over to Mrs. Wong and jumped up to greet her with a kiss that made Mrs. Wong beam. When they had first adopted Hattie, the Wongs worried that she preferred the shelter to home. But they soon saw that it was just a matter of training Hattie to come when she was called. Now they knew that Hattie could have a great time with us and still be very happy to go home with them.

"Thanks again," Mrs. Wong called, waving to everyone as she leashed up Hattie and headed out.

Sasha, Tim, and I began picking up toys while Caley and Taylor played with the remaining dogs. Through it all, Missy continued to stay close to me.

"Wow."

I turned and saw that Mrs. Benson had come in. Today she was wearing an old gray sweatshirt from

Ohio State University and a pair of baggy jeans. She looked like a different person from the woman who had stood in front of our class in neat khakis and a green blouse this morning, but I was surprised to realize I was starting to get used to the casual Mrs. Benson too.

"She's getting attached to you," Mrs. Benson said. "I just saw her following you."

"She was my shadow today," I said. "I think she's starting to feel safer here."

"She's definitely feeling safer around you," Mrs. Benson said. "Honestly, she seems more comfortable with you than she is with me."

For a moment I worried that this might be like Hattie and the Wongs, with Mrs. Benson thinking Missy liked the shelter more than home. But then she looked at me warmly. "Please, tell me how you do it, so I can start helping her feel comfortable around me too."

I let out the breath I hadn't realized I was holding. Mrs. Benson cared about Missy and making her feel safe, not whether she liked the shelter more than home. And really, that was what mattered most.

"I talk to her a lot," I said. "So she gets used to my voice. My brother makes fun of me for talking to dogs, but they really like it and it's fun."

Mrs. Benson nodded thoughtfully. "I could definitely talk to her more. That sounds like a good idea." Then she grinned. "And tell Matt I said to stop making fun of you."

I laughed at that. "Oh, and something else I read," I went on, remembering an article I'd looked at over the weekend. "That it's smart for you to stay close by when she's eating. Not too near, because you don't want her to feel threatened of course. But it said that if you sit a few feet away then the dog begins to connect the good feelings from eating with you."

Mrs. Benson laughed. "Well, I'd like to be thought of with the same affection she has for her kibble."

I laughed too.

"That's a great idea, Kim," she said. "Thank you.

And now I think I'd better get this girl home for some of that kibble."

She bent down to scoop Missy up. Missy's whole body tensed and she cowered slightly as Mrs. Benson gently wrapped her arms around Missy's soft tummy. It was the right way to pick up a small dog, but it was clear from the way Missy stayed frozen in Mrs. Benson's arms that she hated it.

"She doesn't like this so much," Mrs. Benson said regretfully. "But I don't want to try to train her to use a leash just yet, not when she's still adjusting to so much else. So this is how we're doing things for now."

Mrs. Benson said good-bye to the others and they headed out.

"You seem so comfortable with Mrs. Benson now," Sasha said, coming up to me. Her curls were falling out of her ponytail and her cheeks were pink.

"It's funny, when she's here it's not like she's my English teacher," I said. "She's just another dog owner."

"Not to me," Taylor said from the spot on the floor

where she was snuggling with Gracie and Boxer. "She might put on a regular-person costume, but she's not fooling me in that sweatshirt. She's still the scary lady who whips everyone in her class into shape."

"I didn't have her when I was in middle school, but I heard the stories," Tim said. He was playing with Lily and Mr. S.

"She's not so bad," Caley said.

Tim rolled his eyes. "You only think that because you're a genius English student," he said.

Caley smiled. "Well, I can't deny that."

I laughed along with my friends but in the back of my mind I kept picturing Missy, scared stiff in Mrs. Benson's arms. There had to be something we could do to make that better.

The question was what.

8

The next afternoon I slowly climbed the steps in front of Taylor's house. Usually I bounded up them because I was with Sasha and we were coming to hang out with Taylor. But today Sasha was at dance class while Taylor was at photography club, and I was here on my own to meet Anna. And honestly, I was dreading it.

"Hey, Kim," Anna said, after I'd rung the bell. "Come on in." Anna and Taylor looked alike, which was kind of funny because their two older sisters actually were identical twins. It was almost like they had two sets of twins in the family. But though they were both tall with heart-shaped faces, Taylor was all smiles while Anna was generally glaring. And she was so smart she made other people feel stupid without even trying. Which was what had me feeling tense now. But Taylor had been so excited that I knew I needed to try. Plus my mom had gotten me a Blue Orchard hoodie, so the situation was getting dire.

"Thanks for helping me," I said to Anna as I followed her upstairs to her room.

"Hey, Kim," Tasha, one of the twins, said as she passed me on the stairs. She and Jasmine were juniors in high school. They did a bunch of after-school stuff as well as having part-time jobs, so they weren't around much.

Anna's room was kind of what I would have expected: filled bookshelves on every wall, a big desk with a laptop in the middle, a file cabinet, and posters of Einstein and some other serious-looking people who were probably mathematicians who'd invented things I'd never begin to understand. What was I doing here? As soon as Anna realized how bad I was at math she'd probably give up and tell Taylor I was a lost cause.

"You can sit here," Anna said, gesturing to the desk where she'd set two chairs.

I sat down, feeling awkward, and reached into my backpack for my math book, which I handed to her. "We're working on algebra," I told her.

I expected her to start flipping through the book but instead Anna just held it in her hands and looked at me. "Here's the thing, Kim," she said. "In school, math is usually just explained one way. And if you get that way, then you're set. But if it doesn't make sense to you, if you learn a little differently, then you're lost from day one and it's really hard to catch up. Especially if it keeps getting explained the same way that never made sense in the first place."

"Really?" I asked. It had never occurred to me that

maybe it was the explanations that were hard for me, and not the math itself.

"Really," Anna said, nodding. "So the first thing you need to understand is that you're not bad at math. You just haven't been taught math in a way that works for you."

That sounded too good to be true. "Are you sure?" I asked. "Because I think that I really might not be that great at math."

Anna grinned. "Then I'm very excited we get to prove you wrong," she said. "Let's get started."

An hour later I bounded down the steps of Taylor's house, a big grin on my face. Because Taylor was right: Anna was good at explaining math, *really* good. Everything made sense when she broke it down for me, and when it didn't, she found another way to say it that did make sense. She was patient and encouraging and as I walked home in the golden light of sunset, I thought maybe I really did have a shot at convincing my parents that I could do well at Roxbury Park Middle School.

I could smell my mom's mac and cheese before I even opened the front door. It was one of my favorites and the scent of rich cheese and her secret ingredient, paprika, made me realize how hungry I was. "Hi," I called as I came in.

"Hi, hon," my mom replied from the kitchen.

I was about to head upstairs to put my stuff away when my mom came into the entry hall, wiping her hands on her apron. "Good news," she said, her eyes sparkling. "I called Blue Orchard today. They've already gotten your application and we're going to visit next week."

Her words hit me like an unexpected bucket of cold water. "Wait, what?" I sputtered.

"For your tour of the school," my mom said cheerfully. "To check it out for yourself."

The thought of visiting the school made my parents' whole plan to send me there feel real in a way it hadn't before. And that made my stomach clench up tight. "Do I have to go?" I asked.

My mom's smile faded. "Kim, you need to take this seriously. We're talking about your future and what's right for you. And you need to see firsthand how wonderful Blue Orchard is."

"Roxbury Park Middle School is wonderful," I said. "And I already know it's the best place for me because I go there every day." My eyes were starting to itch and my throat felt tight.

"I know it seems that way because it's what you know and where your friends are," my mom said, rubbing my shoulder. "But you have to think about how great it will feel to understand everything in your classes. And how you'll make new friends."

There were no friends like Taylor and Sasha, not at Blue Orchard or anywhere else in the world. And if I went to a school in another town and had to drop out of Dog Club I'd lose them and everything else that mattered to me.

"Oh, I should check on the mac and cheese," my

mom said. "You must be starving. It'll be ready in a couple more minutes." She gave my arm a squeeze and then walked back to the kitchen.

I wasn't hungry, not anymore. The thought of Blue Orchard had stolen my appetite, the same way it threatened to steal everything else that mattered to me.

"Hey, guys," Brianna said, hovering at the edge of our table in the cafeteria. The three of us had just arrived and were digging into lunch. "Is it okay if I sit with you?"

Brianna was looking at Sasha, who glanced at Taylor, then nodded stiffly.

"I wanted to tell you that I'm sorry for what I said about your dog," Brianna said to Sasha as she set down her tray. "I should have kept my mouth shut. My elbow hurt but it wasn't his fault, and it honestly is amazing that he's nearly blind but can do so much." Her voice was earnest and I could tell she really meant what she was saying. "I hope you can forgive me. I should have apologized on the spot, but I was embarrassed."

And this time when Sasha nodded it wasn't stiff at all. "Apology accepted," she said.

Relief spread across Brianna's face as she settled in the seat across from me. "I had a great time at your dog club and I think doggy basketball might be my new favorite sport ever."

"It's pretty much the best sport out there," Taylor said with a grin. I could tell she was pleased that Brianna had made things right with Sasha and I was too. I still wasn't fully sold on her but at least she could admit when she was wrong and try to make it better. That was definitely worth something.

"I brought brownies," Emily said, leaning over to our table with a tin of perfect moist squares.

"Yum, thanks," Sasha said, helping herself to one and then passing the container on to me. "These smell delish."

They really did. I took one, passed the rest to Brianna, and then took a bite. It was like a mini chocolate explosion in my mouth, rich, sweet, and utterly scrumptious.

"Did you make them?" Brianna asked.

Emily shook her head. "No, my sister did," she said. "She and her friends baked them for a sale at the high school today and she gave me the extras."

"They're fantastic," I told Emily.

She smiled and turned back to her friends at their table.

"I wish I had a sister," Brianna said as she broke off a chunk of brownie.

"Me too," Sasha said.

"Same," I agreed, unwrapping my turkey sandwich, which was going to taste very blah after that brownie.

"Are you both only children too?" Brianna asked.

"I am," Sasha said.

"I have an older brother," I said, wrinkling my nose.

"Matt's not so bad," Sasha said. She speared a cherry tomato from her salad and popped it into her mouth.

"Easy to say when you don't accidentally sit on the

dirty socks he left on the sofa," I said.

"I can tell all of you firsthand that sisters aren't so great, either," Taylor said, dipping her spoon in her yogurt. "All they do is boss you around."

Her mention of sisters made me think about yesterday with Anna and then the conversation with my mom afterward. The last thing I wanted to think about now was my tour of Blue Orchard, but Anna had been really helpful and I realized I hadn't told Taylor yet.

"You were right about Anna and math, by the way," I said. "She's an awesome tutor."

Taylor beamed.

Brianna was looking thoughtful and I suddenly realized that I'd revealed the fact I was being tutored. I wasn't sure I was ready for her to know about this, not when I still felt weird about it.

"I had a math tutor at my old school," Brianna said matter-of-factly. "I had issues with fractions and it really helped to have it explained a different way. And also to get the extra practice outside class."

And just like that my reservations disappeared. "Yeah, it helps," I said, smiling at her.

"So you guys, I had a question," Brianna asked in a small voice. "Can I come back to the Dog Club?"

I looked at Sasha, who was frowning slightly, and I knew we were both still just a little unsure of Brianna.

"I'm just so tired of doing nothing all afternoon at the library and my mom doesn't need me at the Pampered Puppy," Sasha said. "And it's really fun at the shelter." She looked at Sasha. "I promise I'll treat your dog like the perfect little guy he is."

Now Sasha grinned. "He's the best," she said.

Brianna grinned back but I saw her twisting up her napkin nervously as she waited for our answer. Taylor glanced at me and Sasha, her brows raised slightly in question. I waited until Sasha had nodded and then I did too.

"How can we deny you the good time that is our club?" Taylor asked. "You can totally come."

Brianna let go of the napkin and smiled. "Awesome."

9

But it wasn't so awesome that afternoon. Mrs. Benson was in a hurry when she dropped Missy off, so I didn't even know the little Yorkie was at the shelter until there was a problem. Caley and Tim were running late, so the four of us were managing all the dogs by ourselves, which normally would have been fine. But today Boxer was extra energetic, and before we could manage to take a group of dogs outside, a food delivery arrived. When the shelter dogs saw the familiar sight of big bags of kibble they went nuts, running and leaping all over the place. The woman carrying the bags jumped back suddenly to avoid getting trampled by Boxer and that's when I heard Missy cry out. The woman's boots were nearly on top of Missy, and Missy was clearly terrified.

"It's okay," I said, rushing over to her.

But Missy didn't even glance at me. She backed away into the other corner, her eyes dull.

"Missy, it's all right," I said, coming closer.

Missy scrambled to back up again but since there was no space behind her, her backside hit the wall. She cried out again.

"Oh no," Sasha said, coming up behind me. "She's really frightened."

"I know," I said regretfully.

"What can we do?" Sasha asked, looking sadly at poor Missy.

"We have to give her some space," I said, stepping away. I hated to do it but I knew it was the best thing for Missy. "Right now she doesn't feel safe, and having anyone too close will just make it worse."

"But she likes you," Sasha said. Mr. S had sensed his owner's distress and came over to press himself against Sasha's legs. She picked him up and hugged him tight.

"She was starting to like me," I said. "But winning her trust is going to take a while. And this was a step back."

Sasha sighed. "That's rough," she said. "I wish we could do something to help."

"Me too," I said, feeling upset that we hadn't protected Missy. But right now there was nothing to do but let Missy get over it, in her own time. And then I could start building our relationship again.

Tim and Caley came in, their hair windblown. "Sorry we're late," Tim said. "There was a bake sale and we had to support the glee club."

Caley socked him in the arm. "It wasn't for glee club, it was for the winter musical. Which I plan to star in." Caley was really into drama and had had the lead in a number of school plays and musicals.

"Whatever," Tim said. "The important thing was that they had great brownies. Which they ran out of, but we did bring you guys some cookies."

"We actually had some of the brownies at lunch," Taylor said.

"Oh, so you guys have an inside connection on all the best baked goods?" Tim joked. "I'll need to work harder to get on your good side so you start bringing some to me."

We laughed as Tim handed around cookies.

"Thanks," I said, stuffing mine in my mouth fast, before the dogs realized there was food in the room.

"These are yummy," Sasha said after she'd finished hers. "You're already starting to get on my good side."

Tim laughed as he grabbed Boxer's Frisbee. "Let's take this party outside," he said.

It had been a while since I'd spent time in the backyard. I'd wanted to stay close to Missy but since I couldn't do that now, going outside seemed like a good option. "I'll come too," I said.

That meant Taylor, Sasha, and Brianna would come too, of course.

The four of us put on our coats and headed out into the crisp, windy day, with most of the dogs following. Only Humphrey, Daisy, Gracie, Gus, and of course Missy stayed behind with Caley.

"You're it," Tim said, tapping my arm the second we got out to the fenced-in yard strewn with colorful fallen leaves.

"Kim's it!" Taylor shouted, starting to run toward the back corner of the yard.

"It?" Brianna asked, confused.

"For dog tag," Taylor explained. Dog tag was another game we'd invented and the dogs loved it. "One of us is it and throws the Frisbee while everyone else runs. The dogs get the Frisbee, then run after us, and whoever they catch first is it next time."

Brianna nodded. "Got it," she said, and then took off running.

I threw the Frisbee toward the side of the yard, but the wind caught it and smacked it into the big oak tree. The dogs, who had been chasing after it, all doubled back while I ran in the other direction. Lily came up with the Frisbee and trotted toward Tim, who stumbled but caught himself as he raced away. All the dogs thought it was super exciting to run after him, and soon the whole pack had joined in the chase.

"Help," he called, laughing, as he passed Sasha. Lily tried to give Sasha the Frisbee but she bolted away, and then all the dogs started going after her.

"This is fun," Brianna announced a few minutes later.

"For you!" Taylor shouted. She was being chased by an exuberant Boxer, who had the Frisbee.

But then she came toward me and Boxer leaped out in front of her, coming right at me. I ran for the back of the yard, the dogs barking and bounding behind. The air smelled like fresh cut grass and leaves, the wind cooled my cheeks, and nothing felt better than racing around after a long day of sitting in a desk at school. Brianna was right—this *was* fun.

"Break time," Taylor gasped a little later, flopping down on the grass. Lily took this as an invitation and settled next to Taylor, resting her head on Taylor's knee. Taylor immediately began petting her.

"Sounds good," Sasha agreed, sitting down next to Taylor. Mr. S, Waffles, and Coco came to lie down too while Boxer, Hattie, and Lily pranced around the yard together.

"I'll go get us a few more balls," Tim said, loping up the stairs of the back porch. We kept a bin full of toys on the porch, but the dogs often brought everything back inside so we were constantly refilling it.

I was thinking I'd go inside too, to check on Missy, when I noticed Brianna trying to pet Hattie. Hattie jerked away and Brianna surprised me by not taking Hattie's clear signal. Instead of backing off she came closer to Hattie, trying to pat her head. Hattie ducked away and then ran across the yard. "What's wrong with

Harriet?" Brianna asked, sounding annoyed.

"Her name is Hattie," I said. "And she's really shy."

"She was a rescue," Sasha added, as defensive as I was of our sweet Hattie. "She was abandoned, so she's skittish with new people."

"She's met me before though," Brianna said, twisting a lock of long black hair around her fingers as she looked across the yard at Hattie.

"Well, you came to the club before but you didn't play with her," Sasha pointed out.

Brianna bit her lip and I could tell she felt bad. "I didn't mean to upset her," she said. "The dogs at my mom's place are different. I guess I'm just not used to dogs with issues."

That really got my back up, but Taylor just laughed. "Dogs with issues are the most interesting," she told Brianna playfully. "Who wants some boring normal dog? There's no challenge in that."

Brianna laughed too and her face softened. "Sorry, guys," she said, coming to sit with everyone. "It makes sense she needs time to warm up, and I'll back off. She's just so cute, I wanted to snuggle with her."

My anger slipped away. I was starting to see that this was just Brianna. She flared up, like a dog with a snarly bark, but after she calmed down she was all smiles, like the same dog wagging its tail. I liked how straightforward she was and how she could own it when she messed up. Plus she'd been really cool about me being tutored. I finally had to admit it: Taylor had been right about Brianna. She really was a good friend.

"I can help you with Hattie if you want," I said.

Bri nodded, so I headed inside for some doggy treats. I checked on Missy as I came into the shelter, but she was still huddled in the same corner and didn't glance my way. So I grabbed a handful of beef-flavored biscuits and went back outside.

Bri and I walked slowly over to Hattie, who wagged her tail as we approached and let me pat her head.

"Show-off," Brianna teased, knowing to stay back a bit this time.

I laughed. "Okay, your turn," I said, handing her a

treat. "Get down low and hold it out to her."

Bri followed my instructions and after a moment, Hattie's appetite won out over her reservations and she took the treat from Brianna. "Now let her sniff your hand," I said.

Bri offered her hand and Hattie sniffed it delicately, then stepped closer to Bri. I passed Bri another treat and after a repeat performance, Hattie pressed herself against Bri's legs.

"The dog whisperer strikes again," Taylor said.

"I think it was the dog biscuits that did it," I said, laughing, as I went to sit down next to her. The grass was warm from the sun and it felt good to sit.

"No, it's you," Bri said in her honest way. "You just get how to be with dogs."

Hattie was practically on her lap now, which made me smile. "With Hattie you just have to take things slowly, let her sniff your hand and choose when she's ready to get closer to you."

"Got it," Bri said, stroking Hattie's long, fluffy ears. Then she looked up at me and grinned. "Thanks, Kim."

"Anytime, Bri," I said.

Her grin widened when she heard me use her nickname.

The porch door opened and Caley came out. "Kim, want to come in and talk about *Tom Sawyer*?" she asked as Tim passed by her with an armful of dog toys.

"Yeah, thanks," I said, standing up. I didn't really want to leave all the fun in the yard, but we were due for a pop quiz in English and I knew I should do all I could to be prepared. Plus I could sit near Missy and start rebuilding the trust between us.

I spent the rest of the afternoon learning more about *Tom Sawyer*, staying close but not too close to Missy and cuddling with Humphrey. Caley still confused me sometimes but I walked home knowing at least a little more about the book. I just hoped it was enough for me to finally do well on one of Mrs. Benson's famous quizzes.

Because my time was running out.

★ ★ ★

"Okay, everyone take out a piece of paper and let's see what you remember about our friend Tom Sawyer," Mrs. Benson said. She stood in front of the classroom in black slacks and light blue Oxford shirt that was perfectly ironed. Her short blond hair was neat and her face had sharp edges as she gave Dennis a look that stopped him cold. He'd been leaning across the aisle to whisper something to Carmen, the smartest girl in the class, but he scrunched down in his seat meekly. This Mrs. Benson, who could probably stop a stampede of bulls in their tracks with a single glare, was nothing like the smiling, warm Mrs. Benson who was so eager to help Missy.

But right now I didn't have time to marvel over how one person could have two such different sides. This quiz was my first chance to show my parents how hard I'd been working and how well I could do in my classes right here at Roxbury Park Middle School.

Taylor glanced over at me and flashed me a covert thumbs-up. Sasha gave me a reassuring nod from her seat. They both knew how much this mattered. My stomach was in knots as I printed my name and the date across the top of the paper, and waited, pencil poised, for the first question.

"How did you do?" Taylor asked, rushing over to me after class.

I shook my head, my eyes watering. "Not so good," I whispered. I'd known a few of the answers, but Mrs. Benson went so fast that anything I needed to think about made me miss what she asked next. Plus she asked things that Caley hadn't talked about. Or maybe she had and I just hadn't understood. Whatever had gone wrong, I now had another failing quiz to show my parents, more proof to make them think that I belonged at Blue Orchard.

"Oh, Kim," Sasha said, wrapping an arm around my shoulders. "It's just one little quiz. You've barely had any time to talk about it with Caley. You'll do better next time, I know it."

But I didn't. My feet were heavy as I walked down the hall, wondering how much longer I'd get to be here, where I belonged.

Because after this, my days at Roxbury Park Middle School were numbered.

10

"So what did you think of the tour?" the head of admissions at Blue Orchard, Ms. Klein, asked me. She wore a sleek suit and her smile was crisp. She was as intimidating as the rest of the school and I sucked in a breath, not sure what to say or how I'd even get words out when it felt like there was a boulder pressing down on my chest.

"It was just great," my dad said. He was all dressed up with a tie and everything.

"We especially loved seeing how classrooms are set up so that students can work in small groups," my mom gushed. She had gone all out too in a blue dress, makeup, and a flowered silk scarf. "We think Kim can thrive in a place where there's more project-based work and individual attention."

"We specialize in that here," Ms. Klein said smoothly.

My parents had told me on the ride over that the one-hour tour would end with what Blue Orchard called an "informal chat." It was where the head of admissions could get to know students and families who applied, and it sounded even more uncomfortable than the wool skirt my parents had bought me just for this meeting.

The skirt itched now as we walked into the sunny admissions office. The hardwood floor was covered with a rug that looked old, but expensive, antique old. The walls had photos of Blue Orchard students, some in class working hard, one with a group hanging out

129

on the lawn, and then a series of shots where students were accepting awards. It didn't do anything to take the boulder off my chest.

"Kim, tell me what kind of student you are," Ms. Klein said. Her hands were folded on her big desk and she leaned toward me, her gaze penetrating.

I shrank back in my chair, which was so puffy I felt like it was squeezing me. "Um, I'm not really sure," I said, my voice squeaky.

My mom shot me a look before turning to Ms. Klein. "Kim is a very hard worker," she said. "She cares about school and takes pride in her assignments."

Ms. Klein nodded, then her gaze went back to me. "And what would you say your weaknesses are?"

I gulped, knowing I had to come up with something this time. "Ah, I study a lot but sometimes my grades aren't so great," I said.

"We believe Kim's grades don't reflect her effort or her full capabilities," my dad added quickly.

"The classes at Roxbury Middle School are too big,"

my mom added. "A student like Kim can get lost there."
I noticed that she was twisting her wedding ring as she
spoke, which meant that she was nervous. Clearly she was
worried I wasn't good enough to get into Blue Orchard,
which made me sink down into the seat even more.

"Some learners need more guidance from a teacher,"
Ms. Klein said.

"Exactly," my dad said eagerly. "That's what we
want for Kim."

It wasn't what *I* wanted, but I bit my lip and kept
my mouth shut.

"Let me tell you more about the offerings we have
for students who need extra help," Ms. Klein said.

My parents both nodded eagerly and I gazed out
the window as Ms. Klein droned on about group work,
teacher office hours, and peer tutoring. I didn't care
how posh the school was, how impressive the students
were, or what kind of help they offered. It wasn't the
school for me, and everything I had seen here just confirmed that.

But as my parents nodded and oohed and ahhed at everything Ms. Klein said, I had the awful feeling that I was the only one who saw this. Because clearly my parents were convinced that Blue Orchard was the place for me.

And I had no idea if I could ever convince them otherwise.

"Hi, Kim," Mrs. Benson said as she and Missy walked into the shelter the next afternoon. Missy was rigid in her arms and when Mrs. Benson set her down, the small dog scuttled into her usual corner and shook herself, as though to get rid of the memory of being held.

Which was exactly what I wanted to talk to Mrs. Benson about. "I read something last night that I think we should try with Missy," I said. As usual it was strange to see Mrs. Benson in her casual clothes, but today it was a good thing too, because the last thing I wanted to be thinking about was that quiz or anything that would remind me of Blue Orchard. I just wanted to enjoy my time with the dogs and forget about the awful tour and the way my parents acted like Blue Orchard was the best school ever.

Waffles came up to greet me and I rubbed his fuzzy head as Mrs. Benson nodded at me to go on. "It talked about how to help dogs feel comfortable on the leash," I said.

"I'm not sure introducing Missy to the leash is such a good idea right now," Mrs. Benson said hesitantly.

"The thing is, it seems like it makes her unhappy to be carried," I said. "And if we could maybe find another way, with the leash, then I think it would help Missy trust you more."

Mrs. Benson looked thoughtful, so I went on.

"The idea was pretty simple," I said. "You just put the leash on and let the dog walk around with it."

Mrs. Benson frowned slightly. "How would that help her?"

"The article said that this way a dog can get used to how the leash feels without having to worry about being led anywhere," I explained. "It's like there are two things a dog has to learn with the leash—how it feels to be attached to something and then how it feels when that something starts steering you around."

Now Mrs. Benson was nodding. "So the idea is to let the dog get comfortable with one part at a time."

"Exactly," I said.

Mrs. Benson looked over at Missy and smiled. "She has her eye on you," she said.

I glanced over and saw it was true: Missy was looking at me. Clearly she had gotten over the scare of the food delivery and was ready to start bonding again. A wave of happiness washed over me.

"Obviously she trusts you, Kim," Mrs. Benson said. "And so do I. So if you think this will help Missy, let's do it."

"Great, thanks," I said, feeling my cheeks warm at her compliment.

"Oh, and I wanted to tell you that staying near Missy when she eats is going well," Mrs. Benson said.

"At first she wasn't sure why I was hanging out in there, but now she seems to like the company. And she's been following me around the house a bit more."

"Great," I said, feeling happy for both Missy and Mrs. Benson. Sure, these were small steps, but they were steps in the right direction.

"So thanks for the tip," Mrs. Benson said. "I'll see you at pickup." She stopped to say hi to Sasha and Taylor and then headed out.

"I'll take some of this crew outside," Caley said. She was petting Boxer, who was so excited he was bouncing each time she touched him.

"I'll come too," Tim said.

They headed out with Boxer, Gus, Gracie, and Coco. Taylor started up a game of tug-of-war with Mr. S while Sasha threw a red rubber ball for Hattie, Daisy, Waffles, Popsicle, and Humphrey. I went over to the supply shelf, where I found a thin light blue leash, and then ducked into the food room for a few doggie treats. I carried both over to Missy and then sat down about two feet away from her.

"I'm happy to see you," I told her in my low, calm voice. Missy didn't look over but her ears twitched. "And I hear you've been having some company while you eat. That sounds really nice." I continued to talk to Missy and after a few minutes she looked over at me, her eyes bright.

"You're a very pretty girl," I told her. "And that coat of yours is looking great." It really was looking healthy. "You know what color would look good with it? Blue." I slowly held up the leash and Missy looked at it with interest.

I held it out to her, slowly, and after a moment she sniffed it.

"It's so pretty I think we should go ahead and put it on you, to see how it looks," I told her, reaching out with my other hand to give her a dog biscuit. I wanted her to have only good feelings about the leash.

Missy crunched down happily on the treat while I inched closer.

"I'm going to attach this to your collar," I told her gently. I gave her another biscuit, then snapped the leash on while she chewed. She paused when she felt it but then kept on eating.

"You have the leash on your collar now," I told her. I walked a few feet away, then crouched down, holding out another treat. "Come on over and see how it feels."

Missy started toward me, then stopped abruptly when the leash came with her.

"Pretty great, right?" I asked her, encouragingly. "Leashes are awesome because when you have one on you can go all kinds of neat places."

Missy looked at me as though considering what I was telling her. I held out the treat. Missy hesitated, then walked over, the leash dragging behind.

"Good girl," I told her happily when she came up and took the treat. I had to hold myself back from hugging her because I knew that would only upset her. But she was so cute and snuggly it was hard.

I spent the next half hour having her walk the edges

of the room, getting used to the leash. And then, when I worried she was overstuffed with dog treats, I decided it was time for a break. "You did a wonderful job," I told her.

"So did you, Kim," Alice said.

I hadn't noticed her come out of her office, but she was smiling at me as she brushed back a lock of hair that had fallen out of her ponytail. She was wearing a pink T-shirt with a cartoon dog lying in a hammock that said "Dog Days."

"You're really making progress with her," Alice said. "I've been watching you and I'm impressed. She's starting to come out of her shell."

Her words made me glow. Alice was amazing with dogs and a compliment from her meant everything.

"Thanks," I said. "I'm hoping to help her learn how to use a leash so Mrs. Benson won't have to carry her around."

"That will improve their relationship," Alice said with a nod. "I know Mrs. Benson is committed to helping Missy, but rehabilitating a puppy-mill dog can be a long and hard process."

"One article I read said that it can take months, if not over a year," I said.

The corners of Alice's mouth turned down sadly. "And that can be very hard on owners, to give for that long and not get anything back."

That made sense. Part of what made dogs so wonderful was how loving they were. So to put so much energy into caring for a dog but not get any love in return could probably be pretty exhausting. I realized it took someone pretty special to get a dog with issues, as Bri would say. Which meant that Mrs. Benson was a pretty special person.

"So anything we can do to bring Missy and Mrs. Benson closer will be good for both of them," Alice said. "And when Missy starts loving Mrs. Benson back, what a reward that will be."

That was true too. Sometimes my mom said that the things we had to work for the hardest meant the most. She said it about homework so I'd never taken it that seriously, but in this case it was really true.

The red rubber ball came bouncing over, followed by Gracie, Gus, and Sasha.

"Sasha, did you get that last voice mail I forwarded to you?" Alice asked as she grabbed the soggy ball and threw it for the dogs.

"Yes, thanks," Sasha said. "I called them back already and put them on the waiting list."

Alice smiled. "It's great that we need a wait list," she said. She bent down to pet Gracie, who dropped the ball at her feet.

"Yes, it really helps keep everything organized," Sasha said. "And maybe in another couple of weeks we can take in another club dog."

"That sounds good," Alice agreed. She tossed the ball for Gracie and then went back to her office.

The back door opened and Tim, Caley, and the rest of the dogs came in. Caley and Tim were laughing at something, and the dogs were overjoyed to be reunited with the humans and pups who had been inside. Boxer nearly knocked me over with his enthusiasm.

"Sit," I told him, and he instantly obeyed.

"Good dog," I said, heading over to his Frisbee. "Now let's play." I sent the Frisbee spinning across the room and five of the dogs raced after it.

"Hey, Kim, want to talk more about *Tom Sawyer*?" Caley asked. Today her red hair was in two braids and she was twining one absently around her fingers.

"Sure," I said. Just thinking about the book reminded me of Blue Orchard and made my stomach lurch like I was seasick. "We're finishing it next week."

"And then we'll have the big test on it the week after," Sasha said. "We can all help you get ready for that."

I brushed off the uncomfortable feeling at the thought of needing so much help and tried to steady my stomach. "Thanks," I said. "That would be great."

★ ★ ★

That night I was starving and ate three helpings of the meat loaf my mom had made. She and my dad told funny stories about a family that had come into the Rox that day and snuck their dog under the table.

"So when the dog jumped up and ate the little boy's pie in one gulp, the jig was up," my dad said.

We all laughed.

"What kind of dog was it?" I asked. I passed my empty plate to Matt, who was clearing the table.

"A little black and white fellow," my dad said.

"It was a cute dog," my mom said. "But even cute dogs aren't allowed to violate the health code."

"What's for dessert?" Matt asked, leaning against the doorway between the dining room and kitchen.

"I brought home some ice cream," my dad said. "Vanilla and strawberry."

"I think there's some left over from Kim's sleepover too," my mom said.

Matt was standing in front of the freezer. "Yeah, mint chocolate chip and coffee," he said, piling up the cartons and bringing them to the table. I got up to get everyone bowls and spoons.

"Kim, I spoke to Ms. Klein at Blue Orchard today," my mom said as we passed the ice cream around. I had just taken a big scoop of mint chocolate chip but suddenly I wasn't feeling as excited about it. "Our application process is completed. Now we just wait to hear if you get in, and we should know soon."

"Oh," I said, pushing the ice cream away. My appetite was gone and now I wished I hadn't eaten so much meat loaf.

My mom smiled and went on. "She also said how much she enjoyed meeting you and how she thought you were the kind of student who could thrive at Blue Orchard."

The seasick feeling was back.

"I have a very good feeling about your chances," my mom finished.

"Um, I think I'm going to go start my homework," I said, pushing back my chair.

"Don't you want your ice cream?" my mom asked, her brows drawing together. I never skipped dessert.

"I'm too full," I said.

"I'll eat it," Matt said, grabbing my bowl.

"I'll come down and wash the dishes in a little bit, when you guys are done," I said, heading upstairs and taking them two at a time. I needed to use every spare second I had to get ready for the next two math tests and the big English test in two weeks, because at this point they were my only hope of staying at Roxbury Park Middle School.

11

The next day it was gray and rainy as we waited at the school's front doors at the end of the day. The exit was bottlenecked because everyone was stopping to put up an umbrella before walking out into the wet afternoon.

"How did the math test go?" Sasha asked as we inched forward, twirling her unopened cherry red umbrella in her hand. Sasha said bright colors always cheered her up on gloomy dark days.

"Pretty good, I think," I said. All my studying last night, practicing the way Anna had taught me, had paid off. "I knew what to do on every question and I had time to double-check all my answers."

"Awesome," Sasha said, beaming.

"Anna's really helped me," I added. "Math makes so much more sense now."

Now Taylor beamed too.

"Hey, you guys," Bri said, squeezing through the crowd. "Can I tag along with you today? I'm in the mood for some doggy basketball."

"Sure," Taylor said as we finally made it through the door and out into the rain.

"Yikes, it's really coming down," Sasha squealed.

We were all wearing rubber rain boots, and good thing, because it was pouring. We hurried to our usual corner and then everyone headed off to pick up their dogs. Bri went with Sasha since she was getting Coco and Gus, the two biggest dogs. I was picking up Humphrey, Mr. S, and Popsicle, and by the time we made it to the shelter, their coats were soaked.

"Here's a towel," Taylor said when we walked in. She passed it to me and then went back to rubbing down Hattie.

"Hey, Kim," Tim called. He and Caley were playing fetch with the shelter dogs and as soon as they were dry, Hattie and Mr. S ran to join in.

Humphrey and Popsicle were more or less dry by the time Bri, Sasha, Coco, and Gus came in. We all helped pat down their fur with fresh towels that Alice brought out.

"I want to coach one of the doggy basketball teams today," Bri announced when we were done.

"Someone's taking over, isn't she?" Tim teased.

Bri put her hands on her hips and grinned. "Does this mean you accept my challenge?" she asked.

"You bet," Tim said, heading to the supply shelf for the laundry basket. "And to show you what a good sport I am, you can have first pick for your team."

They began dividing up the dogs as the door opened

and Mrs. Benson came in, a rigid Missy in one arm, a wet umbrella cradled under the other. She set Missy down and the little dog ran for her usual corner.

"I'll be very happy when you get her feeling comfortable with the leash," Mrs. Benson said. "Carrying a dog and an umbrella in that rain was no easy feat."

"We'll work on it again today," I promised.

"Thanks, Kim," Mrs. Benson said. She waved to everyone and then headed back into the rain.

"Hi, sweet girl," I said to Missy, who gave a quick tail wag at the sound of my voice. "We're going to put that pretty blue leash on you again," I told her, heading over for a few doggy treats and the leash. This time Missy didn't even pause when I clipped it onto her collar, and after getting her to walk around with the treats, I decided it was time to see how she did without the incentive of dog biscuits. The first few times she walked she paused to see what was following her. But when she realized it was the leash dragging behind, she seemed okay with it.

"You're very clever," I told her, squelching down the urge to pat her head. That would come in time, when she was ready. I had to be patient.

The doggy basketball game was getting heated, with Bri and Tim both cheering on their dogs with gusto.

"I think Tim's met his match," Sasha said after Lily had scored the winning basket for her team and Bri pumped her fists in the air and began singing "We Are the Champions."

I laughed. "Totally."

Tim had fallen on the floor in dramatic fashion after the loss and Boxer was jumping on him.

Caley tossed a tennis ball for a group of dogs while Tim got to his feet and began a game of tug-of-war with Boxer. Taylor was playing fetch with Gus, Daisy, and Mr. S, and Hattie was standing by the empty laundry basket looking confused.

"I think Hattie wants to keep playing," I said, about to head over to her. But then Bri walked up to her, moving slowly and holding out her hand. Hattie gave

Bri's fingers a sniff and then came in for a snuggle.

"She's good with the dogs," Sasha said.

"Yeah," I agreed. And suddenly something occurred to me. If I did have to leave the Dog Club because I was going to Blue Orchard, Bri would be able to take my place. She was dependable and everyone, including the dogs, really liked her. I knew this should make me happy; after all, the last thing I wanted was for the club I'd help start to fall apart because I couldn't be there. But the thought of anyone, even Bri, taking my place made my heart twist up in my chest.

"Kim, are you okay?" Sasha asked, looking at me closely.

I shook off the thought. It wasn't going to happen, because I was going to ace these tests and show my parents that I could stay at Roxbury Park Middle School. "Yeah, I was just thinking I should ask Caley for some more help with *Tom Sawyer*," I said.

"Great idea," Sasha said. "I think the test is going to be a tough one."

"All Mrs. Benson's tests are hard," Taylor said darkly. She'd come up behind us. "But Kim, you are going to rock this one."

"I hope so," I said. I started toward Caley but then I heard Missy cry out. I looked back in alarm and realized that I'd stepped on the edge of her leash. Missy was tugging on it, clearly distressed to be stuck.

"Missy, it's okay," I said, going over to take the leash off. But Missy was spooked, and the second she was free she ran over to her corner.

I stood still, unable to believe I'd made such a mistake.

"It's okay, you didn't mean to," Sasha said when she saw my face.

"I know, but this will really set her back," I said. There was a quiver in my voice and I realized my throat was scratchy. Thinking about Bri replacing me, worrying about the English test, and now seeing Missy cowering in the corner had me on the edge of tears.

Sasha put an arm around me. "Kim, you're allowed

to be human," she said gently.

"Yeah, even dog whisperers can't be perfect all the time," Taylor said.

As always, my friends helped. And there was nothing I could do for Missy right now except give her space. So I did the only other thing I could do: I headed over to Caley to talk about *Tom Sawyer*.

Because if I could do well on that test and stay at Roxbury Park Middle School, everything else would be fine.

"So?" Taylor asked as I walked up to her, Sasha, and Bri, who were waiting for me outside the cafeteria. They knew I'd just gotten my math test back, and when I gave a big smile and a thumbs-up the three of them erupted into cheers.

"I got an 89," I said proudly, holding up the paper.

"Go, Kim!" Taylor said, holding up my arm like I was a prizefighter. Which was actually kind of how I felt. I'd never gotten such a high mark on a math test, not since starting middle school anyway.

"I can't wait for your parents to see this," Sasha bubbled as we headed into the cafeteria. Today the steamy air was thick with the scent of pot roast and Brussels sprouts, and I wrinkled my nose as I headed to the sandwich bar to get my sandwich. "They'll know you can do great here and let you stay."

"You know, I think you should wait to show your parents the test," Bri said as we trooped to our table, sidestepping kids leaning out of their seats to yell across the crowded room and moving around to sit with friends.

"Why?" I asked when we reached our table and set our stuff down.

"Well, there's another math test next week, plus your big English test," Bri said, opening the lunch box she'd brought from home and taking out a small thermos. "So if you do well on all three, and show them the results all at once, that will really impress them."

"That's a good point," Sasha said thoughtfully.

"One test isn't as big a deal as three."

"And they'll see that you're really doing well, that it wasn't just a one-time thing," Taylor said. Today she'd gotten minestrone soup instead of yogurt and she was dumping a packet of oyster crackers on top.

"That does make sense," I said. "The only thing is that I have to do well on the other two so it really *isn't* a one-time thing."

"You will," Sasha said firmly, scooping up some tuna from her salad.

"I feel pretty good about the math, thanks to Anna," I said, unwrapping my sandwich. "But parts of *Tom Sawyer* still don't make sense to me."

"You mean like what happens in the story?" Taylor asked.

"No, more like the underlying themes that Mrs. Benson is always talking about," I said. And the problem was still how fast she talked. I didn't have time to process what she said or write it down before she'd gone on to something else. And Caley was great, but she didn't always cover the same things Mrs. Benson did.

"Sasha, are you totally sore from ballet class yesterday?" Dana asked, leaning over from the table next to us.

"Yeah, my thighs ache," Sasha said with a grin. I knew how much she loved dancing and feeling her body growing stronger. "That new dance is a real workout."

"Yeah," Dana agreed.

"But I like it," Sasha went on. "Especially the leaps in the middle."

"I don't know how you guys find energy to leap after school," Emily said. "All I want to do is sit in front of the TV."

"Right, like your mom would ever let you do that," Naomi said, laughing.

"Well, I said that's what I want to do, not what I actually can do," Emily said with a grin.

"Hey, guys," Rachel said, standing up. "I'm going to get some lemonade. Anyone need anything?"

"I'll go with you," Sasha said, standing up and

following her to the buffet area.

I had finished my sandwich and crumpled up the wrapper.

"Are you meeting Anna again before the next math test?" Taylor asked. She was done with her soup and was wiping her hands on a napkin.

"Yeah," I said. "She's been great about finding time to meet. Honestly, with her helping me I'm not even that worried about the next test. It's English that has me stressed."

"Don't stress," Bri said decisively. She had finished the ravioli she'd brought from home and was packing up her lunch box. "That doesn't help. Break the studying down into parts and then take on each part one at a time."

I thought about that. It did seem easier to take on a piece at a time rather than tackle everything at once. "I'll try it, thanks," I said to Bri.

"And we'll talk about it a lot too," Taylor said. "To help you get ready." Suddenly she spotted something over my shoulder and broke out into a wide grin. "It looks like we're celebrating," she said happily as Sasha and Rachel reappeared with a tray filled with cookies.

"What's the occasion?" Emily called from the other table.

"Kim's awesome grade on her math test," Sasha said proudly, setting the tray down in front of me.

"Good for you, Kim," Emily said. "That test was hard."

"Yup, you earned these," Taylor said, gesturing toward the cookies.

I took a chocolate chip one off the top and passed the tray to Bri.

"Thanks, you guys," I said. I meant for more than just the cookies—I meant for how they believed in me and how they wanted to celebrate with me when things went right.

"Anytime," Sasha said. Taylor and Bri nodded.

I could tell they knew exactly what I meant.

12

"Do you want to go in and get Coco while Gus and I wait here?" I asked Bri. She was coming to Dog Club again, which was starting to feel normal, and today she and I were the ones getting Coco and Gus.

"Sure," Bri said, taking the key I handed her and going inside. I could hear Coco barking with delight and Bri speaking in a soothing voice. A moment later they came out and Gus pranced happily at the sight of his friend. We let the two dogs sniff each other to say hello and then headed for the shelter.

"My dad gets home tonight, so I'll have to leave club a little early," Bri said as we crossed Elm Street.

I realized I'd never heard Bri talk about her dad. And I didn't know anything about her mom besides the fact that she ran the Pampered Puppy.

"Where's he coming from?" I asked, stopping to let Gus sniff a mailbox.

"China," Bri said. "He goes a lot for work."

"What does he do?" I asked.

"I have no idea," Bri said with a laugh. "He works for a bank so I know there's money involved, but when he starts telling me and my mom about his meetings we just glaze over."

I laughed too.

"It's nice when he's home though," Bri said wistfully. "I wish he didn't have to travel so much."

Her words made me realize how lucky I was to have my dad around all the time. Not that I felt that way when he was nagging me about homework or cleaning my room, but it sure beat him being out of the country.

"That must be tough," I said sympathetically.

Bri nodded but then she smiled again. "He does bring me pretty great presents from his trips though. And he'll bring ingredients for my mom to make her famous dumplings, the spices we can only get in China. I'll bring some in to share with everyone."

"That sounds awesome," I said. We'd reached the shelter and Bri held the door for me and Gus, then followed with Coco.

Boxer raced up to greet us and Bri and I were quick to release our dogs so they could go play. Hattie ran up to Bri right away. I couldn't help thinking how great Bri was with the dogs and how much everyone liked her. If I left they'd probably be just fine, as long as they had Bri to take my place. But that thought felt bitter and I pushed it away.

"Who's up for dog tag in the back?" Tim asked. He was throwing a tennis ball for Lily, Hattie, and Mr. S, who had already arrived with Sasha.

"Me," Caley said. "I need some vitamin D."

Sasha looked confused. "You left your vitamins outside?"

"She means from the sun," Tim said. "She's trying to sound like a Hollywood star because she made callbacks for the musical."

"Congrats," I said, and Sasha gave Caley a thumbs-up as the door opened and Taylor, Humphrey, and Popsicle came in, followed by Mrs. Benson and Missy.

I headed over to greet them, the blue leash already in my hand.

"Hi, Kim," Mrs. Benson said as she set Missy down. The little dog was stiff as a board until her paws touched the ground and then, instead of running to her corner, she came over and stood near me, her tail wagging.

"Wow," Mrs. Benson said. "Look at that."

My heart was nearly bursting with joy at Missy's show of trust, especially after what had happened with her leash the last time.

"I think that I'll try walking her on the leash today," I told Mrs. Benson. "Want to stay and see what happens?"

Mrs. Benson smiled. "I'd love to see the dog whisperer in action," she said. "I'll just stay out of the way and let you do your work." She headed to the windowsill where Oscar was sleeping and gave him a soft scratch behind the ears as she leaned up against the wall.

I turned my attention to Missy. "It's a big day," I told her, snapping on the leash. Missy didn't bat an eye at the sound. And this time instead of dropping the end of the leash, I kept it in my hand. "Come on, girl," I said, holding a treat where she could see it and starting forward.

Missy took a step, then looked back to see what was going on. But she just saw her leash, something familiar, so she kept walking. I made sure to keep the leash loose as we walked partway around the room. "Good job," I said, handing her a doggy treat.

Missy gobbled it up, and the next time I called her and started walking, she came with me, happily

162

accepting her praise and the treat when we stopped. We did that a few more times, and then I tried it holding the leash a bit more tightly and giving it a gentle tug. The first time I did this Missy stopped in her tracks, but the lure of the dog biscuit won out and soon she was coming with soft leash prompts.

"Okay, that's all for today," I told Missy, giving her one last treat as I took off her leash. "What a good job you did." Missy wagged her tail, clearly agreeing with me.

"Kim, that was amazing," Mrs. Benson said, walking up to me, her eyes shining. "You truly have a gift."

"Thanks," I said, my cheeks warming.

"Have you ever thought about becoming a vet or working with rescue dogs after you finish college?" Mrs. Benson went on. "Because you'd be wonderful at it."

"First I have to pass your class," I said, the words just coming out. "And that's if I can even stay at Roxbury Park Middle School."

The smile slid from Mrs. Benson's face. "What?"

"It's just, my parents are worried about my grades at Roxbury Park Middle," I said, suddenly feeling embarrassed. I didn't want to dump my problem on Mrs. Benson. But she was looking at me steadily, waiting for me to go on. "They want me to go to Blue Orchard Academy."

Mrs. Benson's brows pulled together in a slight frown. "They did ask me for a sample of your work," she said. "I assumed it was for a summer enrichment program, not to transfer schools next year."

"It would be this year," I said, suddenly feeling tearful. "They want me to start in January." Hattie was trotting by with a ball in her mouth, and when she heard how distressed I sounded she stopped and came over to sit against my legs. I bent down to pet her gratefully.

"And you don't want that," Mrs. Benson said.

"No, I want to stay where I am," I said. "If I go to Blue Orchard I'll have to leave my friends. I'll even have to leave the Dog Club because I won't get back here in time."

"Well, Missy would be very disappointed if that happened," Mrs. Benson said. "As would I. I like having you in my class and here at the shelter. Both seem like the right place for you."

"I wish my parents could see that," I said.

"They want you to do well, and I don't blame them for that," Mrs. Benson said. Then her eyes narrowed slightly. "And it's English that's challenging you?"

"Math was too, but I think I get that more now," I said. "But in English I get lost when we talk about themes and motivation and stuff."

Mrs. Benson nodded thoughtfully. "What if I gave you a few tips?" she said. "Some things you can do to break it down a bit more. Because sometimes the problem is simply a matter of taking on too much at once."

That was what Bri had said too.

"That would be great," I said. "If you're sure you don't mind."

Mrs. Benson smiled. "It would be my pleasure," she said. "I love this book and I want you to be able to love it too. And the other things we're reading later this year."

Missy was watching the other dogs play fetch with Taylor, Bri, and Sasha. Mr. S came over and rubbed against my leg and I picked him up and cuddled him close, ready to hear Mrs. Benson's advice.

Mrs. Benson was wearing her old jeans and sweatshirt, but as she began to talk about school, she suddenly looked more like my classroom teacher, even in the casual clothes. She stood a little straighter, her mouth was firm, and her gaze was serious. I was thankful to have Mr. S all snuggly and warm in my arms as she began.

"When you read the text and get to a part that feels important, stop and put a Post-it in the book," she said. "Write a quick phrase saying why you think it matters to the story, and do the same anytime there's something that sparks your interest or emotions. Then when you're done reading, go back and look them all over. Chances are that will give you a deeper sense of the story, and it will help the important things stay in your mind moving forward."

I nodded because that made sense. Sometimes I did forget things that happened at the start of the book, but rereading always took too much time. Rereading Post-its, though, seemed doable.

"Another thing, and this is a big one," Mrs. Benson went on, "is how you take notes during lectures. Don't write down every word I say. Just jot down enough so that when you read it over later you'll remember the main idea."

She must have seen my forehead scrunch up in confusion because she continued. "For example, if I say that one of the themes of the book is Tom's maturation over the course of the story, you shouldn't write that down word for word. Just write something like, 'Theme: In the book, Tom grows up.' Does that make sense?"

"Yeah," I said, thinking about it as I nodded. It really did. I realized that I was always so busy trying to remember exactly what she said that sometimes I didn't even think about what it meant. But thinking about that first and then jotting it down made a lot of sense. And it seemed doable too.

"Thanks, this is really helpful," I said, feeling hopeful about English for the first time in a while.

"It's the least I can do given how much you've helped Missy," Mrs. Benson said with a grin. "Plus I like to see my students do well."

Mrs. Benson shared a few more tips and then headed out. As soon as she was gone, Sasha, Taylor, and Bri crowded around me.

"That was really cool," Taylor said.

"It seemed like she had some great studying ideas," Sasha said enthusiastically.

"Yeah, she really did," I said. "Like I was trying to take notes all wrong, and now I know what to do." I had the same feeling I'd gotten after my first tutoring session with Anna: that something impossible suddenly felt possible.

"Awesome," Bri declared.

The dogs came to see what was going on and Boxer

deposited his Frisbee at my feet. "Thanks for watching the dogs while I talked to her," I told my friends. I threw the Frisbee and watched as the pack of dogs flew happily after it. Popsicle stayed behind and Bri reached down to pet her.

"You know we have your back," Taylor said.

Waffles broke from the pack to get a tennis ball that he brought over to us.

"You belong at Roxbury Park Middle School with us," Sasha added. She bounced the tennis ball and Waffles and Mr. S ran after it. "So we'll do whatever it takes to keep you."

As I threw the Frisbee again I realized that thanks to Mrs. Benson, that just might happen after all.

13

"We have some wonderful news," my mom said that night. We'd just sat down to a tray of lasagna my parents had brought home from the Rox. I'd been excited to dig in, but the way my mom's eyes were shining suddenly had my stomach in knots.

"We heard from Blue Orchard today," my mom bubbled. "And Kim, you've been accepted!"

"I—" I began.

"Congratulations, honey," my dad said, a huge

smile on his face. "We're so proud."

I gulped, my stomach so twisted it was hard to breathe.

"And happy that you've earned a place at this school where we truly believe you can excel," my mom added.

This was a disaster. "Thanks, but—"

"We're going to send in the deposit to hold your spot first thing tomorrow morning," my dad said.

"Please don't!" I said, the words bursting out of me.

My mom's hand froze over the lasagna tray and my dad's smile disappeared.

"I don't want to go to Blue Orchard," I said. Tears pricked my eyes. "I want to stay at Roxbury Park Middle School."

Matt looked at me sympathetically but my mom's mouth was pursed and my dad just looked serious.

"We know it's a big change," my mom said.

"And that switching school midyear is a big deal," my dad added. "So we understand that you're worried."

"It's more than that," I said. "I think I can do well at Roxbury Park Middle School if you just give me a chance."

But now my dad was frowning. "Kim, you've had a few months of school already and it seems to be getting harder for you there, not easier."

"And the problems started last year," my mom added. "We don't want you to feel upset about it, we just want to be sure that you are in a school that can support you as a learner."

"That's Roxbury Park Middle School, I'm sure of it," I said, my voice shaky.

There was a heavy silence and then my mom spoke up. "I think I know what you need," she said.

For a second I felt a glimmer of hope that she'd finally heard what I was saying.

"Blue Orchard is intimidating because you just had one quick tour where you didn't see classes or meet any students," she said, crushing the hope. "But Ms. Klein said that now you can visit for a whole day. They'll pair you up with a host student who will take you to classes, show you the fun kids have together at lunch and after school. That way you can get the inside scoop on what it's like to go there. And then I think you'll be as excited as we are."

That was never going to happen, but my dad was nodding eagerly.

"Great idea," he said. "Kim, once you spend some real time there and get to know some of the kids and teachers, I'm sure you'll feel much more comfortable about the switch."

There was no way I was going to convince them to let me stay at Roxbury Park Middle School, not when they were so excited about Blue Orchard and not when I only had one test to back up my point. So I did the only thing I could think of: I bargained. "Okay, I'll go for a day," I said, and both my parents beamed. "But will you guys wait to send in the deposit until then?" That way I'd buy enough time to take the next math test and the big English exam. And then I'd have something to show my parents.

"That seems reasonable," my mom said, nodding.

"I agree," my dad said.

I let out a breath and then stood up. "I'm going to study," I announced.

"But you've barely eaten anything," my mom protested.

"I had a big snack after school, so I'm not hungry," I said. I couldn't waste a second of study time, not when I finally knew how to prepare for the English test thanks to Mrs. Benson's help. "But I'll come down to clean up." It was my night.

"I've got it," Matt said. When I looked at him he smiled, and I realized that he understood how important it was to me to stay at my school.

"Thanks," I said, feeling a rush of love for my brother.

"Just remember you owe me big," he said with a grin.

Typical Matt. But I was smiling as I headed upstairs

to find some Post-its and start working on *Tom Sawyer.*

This was my last chance to prove that I belonged at Roxbury Park Middle School and however miniscule it was, I was going to make the most of it.

"This is awful," Sasha said, the corners of her mouth turning down. We were in the cafeteria the next day and I'd just told my friends the news.

"Yeah, the worst," Taylor agreed glumly. "I mean, congrats on getting in, but I have to admit I wish you weren't as awesome as you are, so that they'd rejected you instead."

That made me laugh a little.

"The one good thing is that I got my parents to wait a couple of weeks before sending in the deposit," I said, unwrapping my sandwich. My missed dinner had caught up to me and I was hungry.

"Until after the tests?" Bri asked.

I nodded, my mouth full.

"Okay, so if you ace those tests your parents have to

see that you can do well here," Sasha said, pulling worriedly on a loose curl.

I was worried too. Yes, I felt better about English—the trick with the Post-its had gone really well last night—and math was making sense too. But what if the tests weren't enough to show my parents that I was finally caught up?

"And you will ace them," Taylor said, but she was looking anxious too. "Because, Kim, we can't lose you, not here and not at the club."

"I know!" Sasha wailed. "Our club would be lost without our whisperer. And we have all these dogs waiting to get in. We'll have to turn them away if we lose you."

For a second I remembered my thoughts about Bri taking my spot, how good she was with the dogs, and how much my friends liked her. Jealousy pricked me as I looked at her sitting there calmly, delicately spooning up her chicken noodle soup. But then she brushed back her hair and spoke up.

"Don't give up now," she said firmly. "This is the time to fight the hardest, not roll over and abandon everything."

Her words boosted my spirits and I could see Sasha and Taylor looking more hopeful.

"Kim, you do your part and study," she said. "Gather up all the work that shows how well you're doing and get ready to argue like you're a lawyer saving an innocent client from prison."

I nodded obediently.

"We'll quiz you until you know *Tom Sawyer* backward and forward, and if necessary we'll show up on your doorstep and beg your parents ourselves." With that Bri went calmly back to her soup.

"Sounds like a plan," Taylor said, grinning.

"I'm in," Sasha said.

All three of them looked at me. It was like Bri had plugged us in and we were all electrified.

"Let's do it," I said.

★ ★ ★

"So that all makes sense?" Anna asked as I closed my math book. We were finishing up my last tutoring session before the math test, and after today I knew I was ready. Anna had helped me so much that her room had gone from feeling intimidating to feeling cozy. I even liked the posters of the mathematicians—and now I knew their names. Einstein was next to Isaac Newton, and across the room were Benjamin Banneker and Sophie Germain.

"Yeah, it really does," I said, stretching a little. Math was hard work! "Thanks."

"My pleasure," Anna said. "How are things in your other classes?"

"I have a big test coming up in English that I'm studying for," I said.

Anna nodded. "Taylor mentioned that one to me. It's on *Tom Sawyer*, right? An essay test?"

I nodded. "I was confused about the book, but my teacher gave me some study tips last week that have really helped."

Anna rubbed her chin thoughtfully for a moment. "One thing you might want to try on the test is writing a quick outline of how you want to answer the question. That way your essay will be more organized and you'll make sure you say everything you have to say."

I crinkled my brow. "How do you mean?"

"Well, if the question is about the theme of growth in the book, you can start with some statements that answer it and then fill in examples from the text," Anna said, taking out a piece of paper and writing it down as she explained. A few minutes later she had a complete outline, which she handed over to me. "It will take about five minutes, but it's time well spent because after you have it you know what you're writing for the whole essay so you don't have to stop and think."

"Plus it will be organized," I said, thinking about my past essays, which teachers had often called "all over the place."

"Right," Anna said.

"This is great, thank you," I said, folding up the

paper and tucking it in my notebook.

Anna smiled. "I bet you'll do great on the test," she said. "Both of them." She stood up, ready to walk me out.

"One more thing." I dug around in my backpack and pulled out a small box. "I got you something, just to say thanks for all your help," I said.

"Oh, Kim, you didn't have to," Anna said, surprised. "I was happy to do it."

"I know, but I appreciate it so much," I said, handing her the package. "So this is for you."

Anna opened up the box and then gave a cry of delight. It was a picture that Taylor had taken with a timer, one of all four sisters together. She'd given it to me last week and I'd bought a frame to go with it, one that had numbers and math symbols along the chunky wooden edges.

"I love it," Anna said, her eyes shining. She set it on her desk, right next to a big pile of math books. "And if you ever need more help, let me know."

"Thanks," I said as we headed downstairs.

I walked home in the cool evening air, ready for a night of studying. The math test was on Wednesday and the English exam was on Thursday, and I was going to be ready!

14

"So how'd you do?" Sasha asked.

I'd just taken the math test and was surprised to see that she, Taylor, and Bri were right outside the classroom. They must've raced to get here.

"I got a 93," I said, a wide grin taking over my face as my friends whooped and high-fived me.

"One down and one to go," Taylor said as we all walked down the hall together.

★ ★ ★

Sasha, Taylor, and Bri quizzed me on *Tom Sawyer* all through lunch, with help from Emily, Naomi, Rachel, and Dana. At this point I didn't even care who knew I needed help—I just wanted to pass the test. Then I spent the whole afternoon and evening studying. I was about to reread my Post-its for the fiftieth time when I got a text from Taylor. *Time to call it a day,* it said. She was right—I knew how much a good night's sleep helped with a test.

So I turned out the lights and went to bed. I was worried it would be hard to fall asleep but I was out the second my head hit the pillow—all that studying was tiring.

The next morning I felt refreshed and ready. I put on my favorite jeans and the red wool sweater my grand-mother had knit me, then headed to the kitchen for breakfast. Bri had told me to be sure to eat brain food, which she said meant protein, so I was about to see what we had that might count when the doorbell rang.

My parents were already at the Rox serving the

breakfast crowd and I could hear that Matt was upstairs in the shower, so I went to the door.

"Your breakfast is here," Taylor said in a grand voice. She, Sasha, and Bri were standing on the porch and Bri was holding a big thermos.

"It's real brain food," Bri said excitedly as they filed in.

"That sounds so gross," Sasha said. "Like we're going to eat mashed-up brains."

Bri shot her a mock insulted look and Sasha giggled.

"Where are glasses?" Bri asked when we got to the kitchen.

"I'm on it," Taylor said, grabbing four from the shelf in the dining room and setting them on the island in the kitchen.

Bri carefully poured out four servings of something thick and paste colored with a slightly greenish hue.

"Um, what is that?" I asked, trying to sound interested and not grossed out.

But Bri wasn't fooled. "Don't worry, it's not pretty

184

but it's super healthy and it tastes good too. It's vanilla yogurt, flaxseed oil, bananas, and walnuts blended together."

That sounded pretty safe. I picked up my glass and took a sip.

"Oh, and there's kale too," Bri added.

I nearly spit out the drink. Kale was not what I had in mind for breakfast! But then I realized that the smoothie was actually delicious—you couldn't even taste the kale.

"Good, right?" Bri asked.

I nodded and we finished up the smoothies.

Then we headed out to school, together.

"I bet you did great," Sasha said, squeezing my arm that afternoon. The four of us were on our way to Dog Club but my mind was still back in first-period English and the test.

"I don't know," I said, my feet crunching on a pile of leaves. "I mean, I had a lot to say in the essay. I'm just not sure it was the right stuff."

"That's what makes essay tests so tough," Taylor agreed, twisting a braid around one finger. "You have to figure out what you should talk about and then make sure you back it up well."

"I wish Mrs. Benson corrected tests in class right after like Mr. Russo," I said with a sigh. "Waiting until Monday is going to be the worst."

"At least we have the dogs to play with," Sasha said. We'd reached the corner where we separated and we each went to get our Dog Club clients. Today I was getting Humphrey, Popsicle, and Mr. S, and Sasha was right—as soon as I walked into their foyer and was greeted with doggy kisses and barks of joy, I relaxed, at least a little.

It was even better when we got to the shelter and Boxer came over, running so fast he skidded a bit and plowed into me. "I'm happy to see you too," I told him, giving him a hug after I'd unleashed Humphrey and Popsicle.

"Doggy basketball starts in five minutes," Tim

called over the din of running dogs and laughing people. "I'm coaching the winning side."

"Don't be so sure about that," Bri said, walking over. They began picking their teams.

"I'll be the ref," Caley said. "You guys are going to need someone to keep this from getting out of hand. And I mean you two, not the dogs."

Sasha, Taylor, and I laughed at that, but Bri and Tim were too busy starting to coach their dogs to notice.

Sasha went over to cuddle with Humphrey, who was napping in a spot of sun, and Taylor was playing a quiet game of fetch with Waffles, who was in a calm mood. I was about to join them when the door opened and Mrs. Benson came in, proudly leading Missy on her new blue leash.

"Wow," I said, going over to greet them.

When she saw me Missy gave out a happy bark and pressed herself against my legs. I bent down and finally, finally gave her the hug I'd been waiting for since the first day I'd seen the sad little dog come through the door. Missy panted happily, letting me hold her close for a moment. Then she wriggled a bit, letting me know we were done. I stood up as Mrs. Benson unleashed Missy and realized my eyes were a little teary; good tears. It was just so great to see Missy happy!

"She's come a long way," Mrs. Benson said, sounding almost teary herself. "And so much of that is thanks to you."

"I love her," I said, watching Missy, who was now looking at the other dogs as they played. Before too long I knew she'd be ready to join them.

"I love her too," Mrs. Benson said softly. "I know some things will always be hard for her but I think she's truly on her way to leading a good and peaceful life."

I nodded, feeling sad for what had happened to Missy but at the same time thankful that she was with an owner who loved her now. She would be okay and that was what mattered most.

"And now I have a bit of good news for you," Mrs. Benson said with a grin. By the way she straightened up

I could tell this was about school, and my heart started thumping double-time in my chest.

"I had time to do a bit of grading over lunch," Mrs. Benson said. "I know how much this test means to you so I brought it for you now, so you wouldn't have to wait until Monday."

My hands were clammy as I took the paper she held out. There, right on top, was a bright red A. I gasped, then shrieked. Poor Missy looked over in alarm but Sasha, Bri, and Taylor knew a victory cry when they heard one and came rushing over.

"Let's see," Taylor said, and I held up the paper.

My friends cheered and hugged me. I realized we were probably a bit wild for Mrs. Benson, but when I looked at her she was grinning.

"I love to see my students proud when they do well," she said. Then she reached over and squeezed my arm. "Good work, Kim," she said, and then she headed out.

"Wow, that was a real fairy godmother moment,"

Sasha said, looking after our teacher.

"I don't think fairy godmothers wear Ohio State sweatshirts," Bri joked.

"This one did though," I said, gazing down at my A. It was so pretty and bright on top of the page.

Coco and Gus came running over with toys and Taylor quickly took my paper and held it out of the way. "We can't let this get wrinkled," she said. "We want it looking perfect when you show it to your parents tonight."

I nodded. "Good call." I went to tuck the test carefully in a folder in my backpack and then headed back to play with the dogs. The glow of that A was beginning to fade as I thought of what was coming next: the big talk with my parents.

"The hard part is over," Sasha said, coming over and reading my mind like she always did. "If you can get an A on a test like that, convincing your parents to make the right decision will be a piece of cake."

"And you deserve a little fun after all that studying,"

Taylor said. "Which means that you're it!"

She was right. Tonight at dinner I'd do everything I could to get my parents to hear my side of things. But for right now, I just wanted to play dog tag!

15

"Is the table set?" my mom called from the kitchen. The house was perfumed with the scent of zesty pasta sauce and meatballs. "Because dinner's all ready."

"Yes," I called back, absently straightening a place mat. I had a folder on my seat with my three tests in it and as soon as everyone sat down, I'd be ready.

"There's something I want to say," I announced as my dad served each of us from the big steaming bowl of spaghetti. "But first I want to show you these." I pulled out the tests and gave them to my mom.

"Wow," Matt said, leaning over my mom's shoulder. "You got an A from Mrs. Benson—that's amazing!"

He winked and I smiled. It helped to have a cheerleader at the table.

"That is impressive," my mom said as she scanned the essay. Then she looked up. "Kim, you did an excellent job on this." She sounded surprised and I couldn't blame her, not after my last English test.

"And look at the math," Matt said, his mouth full of meatball. "You're rocking that class."

I was going to do all Matt's chores for a week after this—he really had my back tonight.

"That's fantastic," my dad said, looking over the tests my mom passed him.

I waited until he was done and then cleared my throat. "I know you guys want me to go to Blue Orchard so that I can do well at school," I said. My hands were shaky and I clenched them tightly in my lap.

"But these prove that I can do well at Roxbury Park Middle School too."

My mom tilted her head to the side and looked at me quizzically. "What changed?" she asked.

"Well, part of it is that Mrs. Benson gave me some really great studying tips," I said. "They made a big difference."

My parents nodded.

"And I also got a little extra help," I said. "Caley and I talked about *Tom Sawyer* at Dog Club. And Taylor's sister Anna tutored me. She mostly worked with me on math, but she also gave me some great pointers about how to organize my essay answers."

My dad looked back down at the English test. "I'd say she gave you some valuable advice," he said. "This is extremely well organized."

I felt a glow of pride at his words.

"So you went out and got a tutor," my mom said as she twined some spaghetti around her fork.

"Well, just to help me catch up," I clarified. I was

way too nervous to eat.

"Right, but you had issues with math and you figured out how to get the help you needed," my mom said. "Which is wonderful."

"Very proactive," my dad agreed, reaching for seconds.

Proactive had to be good.

"You know, we had something to tell you today too," my mom said. "We got a call from your teacher Mrs. Benson."

"Really?" I asked, surprised.

"She wanted to tell us how well you've been doing recently," my mom went on. "And how impressed she is by all your hard work. She said it seemed like maybe you got off to a rocky start but that now you really have the hang of seventh grade."

If Mrs. Benson had been there I would have hugged her.

My mom looked at my dad and they did their silent communication thing, with nods and frowns. I waited impatiently, eager to know what they were deciding.

"Given these grades," my mom said finally, "and the endorsement by your teacher, we're going to let you decide where you go to school in January."

"Roxbury Park Middle School," I said so fast that the words tumbled into each other.

My mom smiled. "We thought you might say that. You can stay, but on one condition."

I'd been about to cheer but swallowed it back down, hoping the condition wouldn't be something awful.

"We want you to keep on with the tutoring," my dad said. "We were actually going to suggest it but since you've already found someone, it probably makes sense to keep seeing her. And of course we'll pay her."

For a second I felt a pang. I still felt weird about needing a tutor. But then I looked at the tests my dad was holding and realized how much Anna had helped. It felt good to understand what was going on in math class and to do well in English. If it took a little help to make that happen, so what?

"That sounds great," I said.

My parents exchanged one last look and nodded.

"Okay, then it's official," my mom said. "You can stay at Roxbury Park Middle School."

My cheer was so loud that my whole family covered their ears.

But they were smiling.

I ate two big helpings of spaghetti before running upstairs to call my friends. I couldn't wait to tell them the news! And news like this definitely meant a video chat. I set up to dial Sasha and Taylor, adding Bri without even thinking about it. But then I paused.

Bri had been so supportive of me these past weeks. And even though I'd felt jealous at the thought of her taking my place at the club, I knew how great she was with the dogs. I also knew we had a line of dogs waiting to get into the club. I thought about it for a second, then took Bri off my call list. I'd text her later—right now I had something to discuss with Sasha and Taylor.

★ ★ ★

"You guys have the best traditions," Bri said happily. Our sleepover this weekend was at Taylor's house and we were in the kitchen setting up the blender for shakes.

"We really do," Taylor agreed, pulling cartons of ice cream out of the fridge.

"Oh, can I have one too?" Anna asked, walking into the kitchen. She ruffled Taylor's braids, making her laugh.

"Of course," Taylor said. "I know what you like."

She got out the ice-cream scoop and began filling the blender with a mix of vanilla and chocolate.

"You're an awesome sister," Anna told her affectionately, and Taylor beamed as she piled in Oreos.

"And I hear I get to spend more time with you, Kim," Anna said, leaning against the counter next to me.

"Yeah," I said happily.

My parents had called Anna and set up a weekly time for us to meet. Anna would tutor me in math and English and help me out with other classes too if I needed it. And I was finally okay with that. It had been hard feeling like I was falling behind in school and when I looked around, I realized that everyone needed some kind of help. Mrs. Benson needed help with Missy. Alice had needed our help at the shelter. Even my parents needed help from me and Matt when it came to making new dishes at the Rox. Getting help made tough things easier—and that was something to take when it was offered, not push away. So I was proud to call Anna my tutor and thankful to know she was in my corner.

Taylor poured Anna her thick shake and Anna took it gratefully, then headed upstairs. The four of us took turns creating our favorite mixes and a few minutes later we were sitting around the cozy breakfast nook, chilled glasses in front of us.

"Here's to Kim staying at Roxbury Park Middle School," Sasha said, raising her drink.

"Hear, hear," Taylor and Bri said as we clicked our shakes together.

"I think we may have something else to toast, too," I said after taking a big sip of mine. It was frothy sweet perfection, as always.

Sasha and Taylor were smiling but Bri looked confused. "There's more good news?" she asked.

"I hope so," I said, leaning forward. "We wanted to invite you to join our Dog Club, and if you say yes I'd call that great news."

Bri was so excited she squealed. "Yes, yes, yes," she cried out so gleefully that we all laughed.

"Will your mom mind?" Taylor asked, and I knew she was thinking of the Pampered Puppy. We'd all wondered if her mom's business might mean Bri had to turn us down.

But Bri was shaking her head. "My mom is so happy I finally have friends, she'd probably let me join the mafia with you guys."

"We could form a dog mafia," Taylor joked, and we all laughed.

"So it's official," I said happily. "The Roxbury Park Dog Club now has four members."

"And we can finally start letting some of those dogs

in off the wait list," Sasha said, wiping ice cream from the corners of her mouth.

I thought back to just a few weeks ago when Sasha and I didn't know if we trusted Bri, Missy was still a terrified puppy, and I was still struggling in school. A lot could change in a few weeks. Especially when you had something as special as the Roxbury Park Dog Club.

"Here's to the club," I said, lifting my glass.

"Hear, hear," my friends echoed happily.

Brianna is thrilled to be the newest member of the Roxbury Park Dog Club. But is there room for her in Taylor, Kim, and Sasha's friendship trio—or will she be stuck feeling like a fourth wheel?

1

"Hey, Bri," Taylor said to me somewhat breathlessly as she came into our locker alcove. Elbowing through the crowd at the end of the day at Roxbury Park Middle School could leave a girl winded like that.

"Hey," I replied, happy to see her. Which was a big change: Not so long ago Taylor had been my number one enemy. I'd been jealous of how easy it was for her to be the new girl at the start of the year, becoming best friends with Kim and Sasha, two of the nicest girls in seventh grade, and helping them start their Dog Club. I'd been new the year before and still felt like an outsider, so seeing Taylor fit in that smoothly made me mad. Some people keep their angry and jealous feelings to themselves, but not me. I spoke up, especially when I was upset, and sometimes I didn't think before I started talking. That wasn't a good idea because some pretty mean things came out. Taylor saw through all that, though, which is just one example of how awesome she is. And ever since, I've really been working on thinking before opening my mouth. I don't want to be the mean girl ever again.

"You ready?" Taylor asked. She was stuffing books into her backpack.

"Yeah," I said, brushing back a stray wisp of my long black hair. I liked playing around with creative hairstyles and today I had a sock bun that I'd rolled up carefully this morning. It sat like a shiny fat doughnut on top of my head, making me look tall.

"Let's go," Taylor said with an easy grin, leading the way out of the alcove. She had to maneuver around kids hanging out talking as they packed up for the day. Before, I'd linger too, but now I had a place to go, and I was eager to get there. Taylor was too. Who wouldn't be excited about two and a half hours of play with the cutest dogs in all of Roxbury Park?

We just had one more stop to go before we'd be on our way.

"I hope Kim did well on that math test," Taylor said. The beads in her braids swung around her face as she spoke. The day before she'd gotten new ones, a mix of lavender and turquoise that looked great with her dark brown skin and big brown eyes.

"Yeah, me too," I said. Our friend Kim was a genius when it came to dogs—the Dog Club was her idea and everyone called her the dog whisperer because of the way she understood and trained pups of all shapes and sizes. But math and English tripped her up, and we'd had a scare when it looked like her parents wanted her to change schools to improve her grades. However, with the help of Taylor and Sasha, Kim had set up tutoring sessions with Taylor's sister Anna, and all of us quizzed her before exams. So far it was working great and when we rounded the corner, I could see her grinning as she chatted with Sasha in front of her locker.

"Kim aced the test," Sasha told us gleefully as we came up to them.

"Awesome," Taylor said, raising her hand to high-five Kim.

"Yeah, that's great," I echoed, not sure if I should high-five too. I knew that Kim and Sasha accepted me as part of their group; after all, they asked me to join the Dog Club and that showed how much they trusted me, which was great. But I had to admit there were still moments when I felt a little like a fourth wheel when the four of us were together. You'd think a fourth wheel would even everything out, but the three of them had inside jokes and memories all their own. And there was an easiness between them that sometimes felt like an invisible barrier, with them on the inside and me on the outside. Still, I was thrilled to be part of the gang and excited for our afternoon at the club. And I hoped that at some point that barrier would come down and I'd be fully on the inside too.

"Thanks, guys," Kim said, her brown eyes bright as she smiled. "I couldn't have done it without your help. And of course Anna's."

Anna was one of Taylor's three older sisters and a math genius. She and Taylor hadn't always gotten along, but lately they were close as could be and Anna had really come through to help Kim.

"Anna's the best," Taylor said proudly. "Are you guys ready to go? The dogs are waiting."

"Then let's get moving," Sasha said cheerfully. Her brown curls were pulled back in a braid and she moved gracefully, probably because she was a star dancer at the school where she studied ballet, tap, and jazz. "Bri, is it your day to get Mr. S? Because I need to give you the key to our house. I had to use the spare yesterday and I forgot to put it back in the hiding place under the plant box."

Sasha was kind of scatterbrained, but she was so good natured about it that it didn't matter. And her cheeks glowed a healthy pink every time she talked about her dog, Mr. S. Not so long ago he'd lived at the Roxbury Park Dog Shelter, where Kim, Sasha, and Taylor had started the Dog Club, both to help owners who worked all day get exercise and attention for their pets, and to raise money for the shelter. But Sasha had fallen in love with him and managed to talk her neat-freak mom into adopting him. Now he had a home with Sasha and came with us to the club to see all his old pals a few times a week.

"Yes, I'm getting Mr. S, Humphrey, and Popsicle," I confirmed. One of the perks we offered Dog Club customers was pickup service. For owners with full-time jobs, the club was the perfect way for their dogs to get a good workout and lots of love and doggy company while they were at work. And for a small additional fee we'd get their dogs on our way to the shelter.

Sasha handed me her key and I put it in my pocket. We wove through the crowd and finally made it out into the brisk fall afternoon. There was a chilly wind, but the sun was warm on my face as we headed into town, our feet crunching on recently fallen leaves. Autumn had definitely come to Roxbury Park.

"I'm getting Coco and Waffles," Taylor said, "since I got Gus and Hattie the last time." Waffles was a shelter dog recently adopted by the Datta family, who had immediately signed him up for the club. Waffles clearly loved his new home but was always happy to see his old friends at the shelter.

"Sounds good," Sasha agreed. We tried to rotate pickups with the exception of one dog.

"How's Missy doing with the walk to the shelter?" I asked Kim. Missy was a new club dog and she actually belonged to our English teacher, Mrs. Benson, who was the strictest teacher any of us had ever had. We were shocked when she showed up at the shelter in jeans and a T-shirt like a regular person, needing help with her new dog. Missy had been rescued from a puppy mill where she had been badly mistreated. She had been like a shadow, scared of everything and cringing whenever anyone got too close. But Kim the dog whisperer had worked her magic, while Mrs. Benson had patiently showered Missy with love, and the little Yorkie was finally coming out of her shell.

"She's doing great," Kim said with a grin. "She loves all the smells on Main Street."

"Like Sugar and Spice?" Taylor asked. Sugar and Spice was the candy store in town and it smelled like chocolate, cinnamon, and strawberries every time we passed. It made my mouth water just to think about it.

"Actually Missy really likes the garbage can on the corner in front of the bank," Kim said, laughing. "She's into two-day-old sandwiches and crusty bits of doughnut."

"Gross," Taylor said, making a sour face that cracked all of us up.

"You should see Mr. S dig into his Buddy's Beef Stew," Sasha said, wrinkling her nose. "Just opening the can kills my appetite for hours, but he acts like it's the tastiest meal ever."

"What does your mom feed the dogs at the Pampered Puppy?" Taylor asked me. "Do they get gourmet dog food?"

Her tone was light, but I felt my stomach tighten at her words. "Um, yeah," I said. "But it still smells pretty gross." The organic fresh minced meat used at the Pampered Puppy actually smelled fine, but I didn't want to make a big deal about it. My mom ran a dog spa that was pretty much a fancy version of our Dog Club. But where our dogs just played and had fun, the dogs who came to the Pampered Puppy got training and each one had an individualized exercise program, as well as regular grooming sessions and carefully planned diets. It was great for people who wanted their dogs obedient and spotless at the end of the day. But I was a lot more comfortable at our Dog Club, where owners just laughed if their dogs were revved up and a bit on the muddy side at pickup.

"Is the new dog coming to Dog Club today?" I asked, wanting to change the subject.

"Yes," Sasha confirmed. She handled all the clients who came to the club, while Kim wrote entries in our blog, the Dog Club Diaries. Taylor took photos for the blog, and recently for a newspaper story that had gotten us more clients than we could handle. We now had a waiting list and one lucky dog had just gotten off it. "Her name is Jinx and she's coming in for her visit today. Her owners say she's mischievous—hopefully she's not another Sierra."

The three of them laughed and I tried to join in. Sierra was a dog who'd been too wild for the club and caused all kinds of problems. I wasn't part of the club then, though, so it was one of those fourth-wheel moments. At least I knew about the visits. Now when a dog wanted to join the club they had an initial visit, to see how they got along with the other dogs and if they were a good fit for the loose, easygoing culture of our Dog Club.

We'd reached the corner where we separated to get our dogs.

"See you guys in a little bit," Sasha called as she and Kim headed straight, while Taylor turned left and I turned right down Spring Street. Sasha and Kim lived a block and a half down, and the Cronins, who had been the first Dog Club members, were right next to Kim's house. I headed to their house and as soon as I slipped the key into the lock of the front door and opened it, I heard a dog let out a happy bark.

"Hi, Popsicle," I said warmly, bending down to pet the black and white puppy with floppy ears. The Cronins had adopted Popsicle from the shelter and like all the dogs she loved her time in Dog Club with her pals.

"And hello to you too, Humphrey," I said to the basset hound making his way slowly into the front hall. Humphrey was a typical basset and didn't rush for anything except food. When he reached us he fell over onto one side, breathing heavily, as though the walk from the living room had exhausted him.

"You are one lazy pup," I told him affectionately, not meaning a word of it. I stroked his silky ears and he let out a contented sigh.

After a little more snuggling, I grabbed their leashes and buckled them on, and we headed over to get Mr. S. When I first met Mr. S I was confused by the way he sometimes ran into things. I was actually a little rude about it after he banged into my elbow, but Sasha, protective doggy mom, set me straight fast. Mr. S, a fluffy white Cavachon, was nearly blind. And considering that, it was amazing how well he got by. Now I loved him almost as much as Sasha did, and seeing him race about in happy circles when the dogs and I arrived to get him made me smile. I bent down and hugged him. Mr. S rewarded me with a kiss and then rushed to romp with his friends.

"Okay, guys, let's get this show on the road," I told my pack of three. Sasha was supposed to leave Mr. S's leash on a hook by the door, but as usual it wasn't there. It took me a minute, but I soon found it thrown over the hall chair, where Sasha had probably tossed it after walking Mr. S this morning. Mr. S stood still while I snapped the leash onto his collar and a minute later we were on our way.